Billy Bunter of Greyfriars School

Billy Bunter of Greyfriars School

Frank Richards

Edited by Kay King and
illustrated by Victor Ambrus

QUILLER PRESS
LONDON

Quiller Press Ltd,
11a Albemarle Street,
London W.1.

First published original edition 1947; this edition 1982

Copyright © 1982 text by Frank Richards and Kay King
© 1982 illustrations Quiller Press Ltd

Cover design and all illustrations by Victor Ambrus

ISBN 0 907621 05 8

Production in association with
Book Production Consultants,
Cambridge

Printed in England by
The Burlington Press (Cambridge) Ltd.,
Station Road, Foxton, Cambridge

Contents

Chapter 1

Bunter Knows!

'Bunter!'

Mr Quelch's voice was not loud, but it was deep. Every pair of ears in the form room heard it—every pair, that is, but one. Billy Bunter's fat ears must have been closed, for he didn't answer.

This was the second time that Quelch had called Bunter's name, and the other members of the Remove stirred uncomfortably, one or two of them risking a glance at the fat Owl. To ignore Quelch was to risk life and limb, and yet the Owl simply sat at his desk, staring silently at his form master through his large, round specs.

'Bunter!' This time Quelch's voice was louder and deeper.

'Third time lucky!' Bob Cherry whispered to Frank Nugent.

'Did you speak, Cherry?' snapped Quelch.

'Oh!' Bob was startled. He hadn't meant Quelch to hear. 'Oh! Well, I—I—er——'

'You will write fifty times that you must not talk in class. Hand the lines to me this evening.'

'Yes, Mr Quelch,' said Bob, subdued.

There was total silence in the form room. No one wanted to risk Quelch's wrath. Harry Wharton, who had been going to hiss a warning to Bunter, closed his lips. Johnny Bull changed his mind about kicking the back of the fat Owl's chair, and Frank Nugent decided not to drop a book on the floor in an attempt to jerk Bunter into activity.

'Bunter!' said Mr Quelch yet again, and this time his voice was very loud and very deep indeed. It echoed round the form room, and floated out through the open window and down into the quad, but it had no effect on William George Bunter. He sat where he was, just gazing at Quelch, a look of indifference on his fat face. A ray of sunlight from the window was reflected on his big spectacles, making them gleam like car headlamps, so that his form master couldn't see that Bunter's eyes were closed. The warmth and the drowsiness of the afternoon, combined with the drone of Quelch's voice, had been too much for Billy Bunter. He had dozed off.

Anyone else would have snapped to attention at the sound of Quelch's voice, but Billy Bunter wasn't quite like anyone else. There were quite a lot of things that he wasn't good at. He wasn't good at games, and he wasn't good in class. He wasn't even good at simple things like telling the truth, but when it came to sleeping, he was quite brilliant.

Quelch gazed at him, his expression growing blacker by the second. 'Bunter!' he roared.

Although the fat figure didn't stir, his mouth opened as if in reply. His lips trembled, and then a long, low snore rumbled round the room. The fat Owl usually snored when he slept, but up till then he had been sleeping quietly. Now, having started, he made up for it. He snored as he breathed in, and he snored as he breathed out, his whole body quivering as volcanic noises erupted from his throat.

'Bless my soul! the boy is asleep!' said Quelch, astonished. One or two boys laughed, but a furious glance from their form master silenced them. 'Skinner!' he ordered. 'Wake Bunter up!'

Skinner's eyes gleamed. Anyone else would have given the Owl a shake, but there was streak of malice in him. He grabbed one fat ear and gave it a good hard pinch.

'Yarooo! Ow!' Bunter was awake in a flash. 'Leggo my ear, you beast! I say, you fellows—ow—wow! Ouch! I say, tain't rising bell!' He jerked his ear free, and blinked around, clearly unaware that he was in class instead of in bed. 'Ow! Beasts! Tain't time to get up!'

'Ha, ha, ha!' yelled the Remove.

'Bunter!' thundered Quelch.

'Oh, lor'!' The Owl boggled as he realised where he was. He blinked at Quelch in terror. 'Oh! I—I say, I—I wasn't asleep, sir! I—I heard every word. Every sis—sus—syllable. Didn't miss a word.'

'You were asleep, Bunter!'

'Who? Me? Oh, not me, sir. I—I had my eyes shut because—because I listen better that way. I—I never missed a word.'

'Indeed? You heard what I said, Bunter?'

'Oh, yes, sir! It—it was so—so interesting,' groaned Bunter.

'Good. Now Bunter, as you know, I was talking about the royal oak. Perhaps you will give me your version of it.'

Bunter blinked at him. He couldn't remember very much about the beginning of the history lesson, but he had a hazy idea that it was something to do with some civil war or other. He didn't know that Mr Quelch had told the story of the battle of Worcester and how the future Charles II had escaped capture by hiding in the branches of an oak tree—the royal oak.

'The—the Royal Oak, sir?' Bunter was puzzled. The only Royal Oak he knew anything about was a public house in the Courtfield road. He'd seen it often enough, but why Quelch was going on about it was beyond him.

'That's right. What do you know about it?' Then, as Bunter remained silent, Quelch said. 'You know what it is, don't you?'

'Oh, certainly, sir.' Bunter was relieved. For once he was able to answer a question. 'But—but I've never been in it, sir,' he said, virtuously.

Mr Quelch clapped a hand to his head. 'What are you talking about, Bunter? What do you mean—

you've never been in it?'

'Not me,' said Bunter quickly. 'Wouldn't. Besides, it's out of bounds.'

'Out of bounds!' repeated Quelch.

'Anyway, my father wouldn't like it. I've—I've always walked straight past it. Never even looked inside.'

Quelch looked at him blankly. 'Are you being impertinent, Bunter? Now tell me. What is the royal oak?'

'It's—it's a pub, sir,' stammered Bunter. 'You know, a—a—public house, sir.'

As the Remove burst into gales of laughter, Bunter blinked at them indignantly. 'I'm right. It's a pub, that's what it is.'

'Silence! That is enough!' He turned to the fat Owl again. 'Are you out of your mind, Bunter?'

'But—but you must have seen it yourself, Mr Quelch. It's got a sign. You know, a picture of an oak tree. It——'

'That will do, Bunter! You will write a hundred lines.'

'Oh—oh! But—' Bunter was dismayed. That beast Quelch was being unfair, that's what he was. He'd answered the question, hadn't he? He'd got it right. The Royal Oak was a pub, he knew it was.

Mr Quelch glared at him. 'You will write one hundred times that the future Charles II hid in the royal oak after the battle of Worcester.'

'But——'

'And if you utter another word, I shall cane you.'

Bunter didn't speak aloud since Quelch was looking positively dangerous, but he felt resentful and indignant. He'd given the right answer, and now he was being punished for it. Life just wasn't fair.

Chapter 2
Many Hands Make Light Work

'I say, you fellows!' A fat face peered round the door of study no 1.

The Famous Five, who were having a drink before going down to the nets for cricket practice, looked up.

'How did you know that Frank had made some lemonade?' demanded Bob Cherry.

'But I didn't.' Bunter beamed at them as he entered the room. 'Still, I don't mind having some.'

'Oh, all right. Go and get something to drink out of,' said Bob. 'Trot off and find your best jewelled goblet. We're a bit short of cups at the moment.' He wasn't exaggerating. The Famous Five had recently had a smashing time and they were reduced to two cups, neither of them with a handle, a chipped mug, a jam jar, and a small jug.

'I can manage.' Billy Bunter had no intention of going to his study. Why, those greedy beasts might finish the lemonade off before he got back.

He seized the jug of lemonade in his fat hands, lifted it to his mouth and gurgled away. Five pairs of eyes watched the level of the lemonade dropping as it disappeared into that capacious mouth. The Owl, however, was unaware of those accusing eyes. Only one thing mattered to him, and that was the refreshment of the inner Bunter. There were more loud gurgles, but eventually he was forced to pause for breath.

'Don't mind us, Bunter,' said Frank, sarcastically.

'Righto, Frank,' said Bunter happily, and tilted the jug yet again. At last, he put it down. 'Pity there isn't any more. That was quite good. Not up to the standard of Bunter Court, but you couldn't expect that, could you?'

Harry Wharton laughed. 'Not really.' He turned to his friends. 'Shall we get down to the nets?'

'I say! Hold on,' said Billy Bunter, hastily. 'What about me? I'd like to get in some practice.'

'We're not stopping you,' remarked Bob. 'I dare say Hurree will send you down a ball or two.'

'I shall be only too pleased, my dear Bunter,' said Hurree Jamset Ram Singh, 'but I hope you'll let me get a glimpse of the wicket. I should hate to spread-eagle you instead of the stumps.'

'What? Spread-eagle my stumps!' said Bunter, contemptuously. 'I can stop anything that you send down, Singh. To tell the truth, I don't think much of your bowling. You try, but you don't bowl like I do.'

'You can say that again,' said Johnny Bull. 'Hurree wouldn't be in the team if he did.'

'Oh, I say, Bull, that's a bit much!' said Bunter, indignantly. 'You'll eat your words when you see me at the nets—but I've got a bit of a problem. Quelch wants those lines. I can't do both. Rotten, isn't it, when I'm so keen to play? I've got a jolly good mind to skip them.'

'And then Quelch will make you skip,' warned Bob. 'Our Henry isn't too pleased with you right now.'

'It wasn't fair. He's a rotten mean beast. I go and give him the right answer, and he goes and gives me lines.' As the Famous Five roared, he blinked at them. 'That's right! Cackle, cackle, cackle, that's all you can do. But it ain't right, talking about pubs in a history lesson.'

'Ha, ha, ha!'

'Look what he's told me to write. All that bosh about a king hiding in a pub after a battle about some Worcester sauce—' He looked scornfully at Bob Cherry who was doubled up with laughter. 'What are you hooting for?' He returned to his grievances. 'I bet he didn't do anything of the kind. Quelch don't know that much about history if you ask me—a bottle of sauce——'

'Not a bottle of Worcester sauce, you ignorant idiot!' shrieked Bob. 'It was the battle of Worcester, not a bottle of Worcester——'

'Oh? Sure?' asked Bunter, suspiciously.

'And he hid in a tree and not in a pub—an oak tree, the royal oak,' added Harry.

'Oh!' A glimmer of understanding appeared on the Owl's face. 'Think so?' As they nodded, he went on, 'But there are still those beastly lines. How many will you do for me?'

'You lazy hound!' exclaimed Bob. 'I've done mine. You could have polished off yours if you'd got down to it.'

Billy Bunter ignored this. He looked at Johnny. 'How many can you manage, Johnny, old man?'

'None!'

'None? That's not friendly, Bull. Still, you don't mean it. You won't let a pal down. I've worked it out,' he said eagerly. 'There are six of us, so if we all did twenty five, that would make a hundred.'

'Oh, my hat!' hooted Bob. 'How many each?'

Bunter thought again. 'Ah, I made a mistake, but I've got it right now. Six twenty's make a hundred. Now, what about it,' he said, briskly. 'It won't take long. You're always saying that I try to dodge cricket——'

'So you do, you fat frowster!' growled Johnny.

'Well, I ain't dodging it now,' said Bunter, triumphantly, 'and it ain't even compulsory today. You'll all see how keen I am on cricket if you'll help me out. As soon as we've done them, I'll come down to the nets.'

The Famous Five hesitated. It wouldn't take long, and they ought to encourage him if he wanted to play cricket. Bunter beamed. 'Let's get down to it. Now you'll have to try and write like me——'

'Like a drunken spider,' said Frank.

'That's not funny,' said Bunter, reprovingly. 'No, you've got to be as neat as me. Why,' he added in a burst of generosity, 'I'll even do some myself. I mean it. No one can call me lazy.'

'Oh, all right,' said Bob Cherry. They helped each other out from time to time, and the fat man seemed to be a deserving case for once.

'Good. I'll start the beastly thing and you can carry on. Mind your spelling, though. Quelch might smell a rat if you get it wrong. You copy what I write.'

They gathered round as he scrawled on a piece of paper. 'King Charles II hid in the royle oke after the battel of Wooster.' He looked at it proudly. 'There you are!'

'You want us to do it like that? That exact spelling?'

'Eh? What? Course I do. I don't want to boast, but spelling's one of my strong points.' There was another burst of laughter. 'Stop cackling. You're wasting time. Get your heads down or we won't get in any cricket.'

'Okay, fat man,' said Harry. 'We'll do it your way. It'll be just what Quelch expects.'

'Don't forget the blots and smears,' grinned Bob. 'He'll expect those as well.'

'Stop yapping,' said Bunter, sternly. 'Just get on with it.'

They did. They sprawled the lines, smudging the ink from time to time. What with that and the spelling, Quelch would certainly think it was the fat Owl's work. When they had finished, Bunter collected the papers.

'I'll nip down to Quelch,' he said. 'I'll catch you up. I won't be a tick.'

The Famous Five went down to the changing room and waited for a short time, but Billy Bunter didn't appear. 'Let's get on,' said Johnny. 'He can follow.'

'It's going to be a bit of bore with that fat freak around,' Harry said, 'but if he's getting keen on cricket, it'll be worth taking a bit of trouble with him.'

But as it happened, they didn't have to. The Owl's sudden enthusiasm for the game disappeared just as quickly as it had developed. While they were playing, Billy Bunter was sitting in the common room, his ample figure firmly planted in the most comfortable armchair, and he was in a state of fat and lazy satisfaction.

Chapter 3

Jam For Bunter

'Stand and deliver!'

'What do you mean, Bob, old chap?' asked Billy Bunter.

'What have you got there?'

'Me? Nothing, old man, nothing at all. Move over, you lot. I'm in a bit of a hurry.'

The Famous Five remained where they were on the landing so that he couldn't escape down the stairs. They were suspicious. Bunter's clothes were tight and filled to bursting point by his plump figure so that the bulge beneath his blazer was obvious to everyone. There was something else that was odd. Usually he moved like a weary snail, but they had seen him coming along the passage at quite a lick.

'I say, you fellows, let me pass,' squeaked the Owl. 'I—I've got to see Quelch. Mustn't keep him waiting.'

'Quelch?' asked Harry Wharton.

'Yes, old chap. Mustn't keep him waiting.'

'That's funny. He's just gone out.'

'Out? Who? Quelch? Did—did I say Quelch.

I—I—slip of the tongue. Wingate, that's who I meant. Let me pass. Can't keep the school captain waiting—must get to his study.'

'I shouldn't bother,' said Frank Nugent. 'He's on Big Side playing cricket.'

'Oh—er—that is, not him. Dr Locke, that's who wants to see me. Sent for me specially. Lemme pass. Won't half be a row if I keep the head waiting.'

He tried to squeeze past the juniors, and gave a startled yelp as his bulge began to slip. 'Whoops!' he cried, and clutched wildly at it. Although he managed to conceal it again, he was too slow. They had seen what it was.

'Ha, ha, ha!' roared Bob Cherry. 'Taking the head jam for his tea, are you?'

'Oh! Yes! No! I—I——'

'Whose is it?' demanded Johnny Bull.

'Mine!' shouted Bunter, indignantly. 'Wouldn't touch another fellow's jam. Not that it is jam. It's—it's ink, that's what it is.'

'Smithy got a parcel from home today,' remarked Bob. 'It had jam in it. You fat brigand——'

'Tain't! roared Bunter. 'I wouldn't touch Smithy's jam. Didn't know he'd got any. Didn't see Gosling giving him a parcel and it wasn't in his study when I looked—not that I was there. Look, I've got to see Quelch—I mean Wingate—that is, the head. They're waiting on the playing field——'

Bob turned as he heard footsteps on the stairs towards the landing. 'You've come at the right moment, Smithy.'

Vernon-Smith glanced up. 'What's going on?'

'A daylight raid,' said Bob, briefly. 'You'd better see if your jam is still in your study.'

Smithy eyed the bulge beneath Bunter's blazer. 'You fat freak!' he said, fiercely. 'Have you pinched my jam?'

Billy Bunter shifted nervously. 'No, Smithy.

'HAVE YOU PINCHED MY JAM?'

Nothing under my blazer, and anyway, it's only a bottle of ink. I—I say, let me pass.'

'If that's my plum jam——'

'No, no,' said Bunter hastily. 'This bottle of ink is apricot jam. No, this jar of apricot is plum ink.' He became even more confused. 'You—you go and look in your study, Smithy. Your jar of jam's on the table, just where you left it.' He turned to the Famous Five. 'Go and help him instead of blaming me.'

'Ha, ha, ha!'

'And I'm taking this bottle of jam down to the Rag to fill Quelch— I—I mean, I'm taking this jar of rag to Quelch to see the head—Ow! Leggo my neck, you beast!' howled Bunter as the Bounder grasped him. 'I tell you I haven't got your jam. Don't believe you had any. Wasn't in your study when I looked, and I left it on the table—never touched it! Wouldn't. Ouch! Leggo!'

'We'll see,' said Smithy, grimly. As he shook Bunter like a jelly, the Owl sagged at the knees, but still he clutched at his bulge in a desperate effort to stop it from slipping.

'Stoppit!' howled Bunter, but the Bounder didn't. He was as determined to see the Owl's booty as Bunter was to keep it hidden, and so he went on shaking.

'Oooogh!' spluttered Bunter. 'Leggo. I say, make him leggo, then you can have some jam.'

The Famous Five laughed as Smithy scowled and shook the fat Owl again. There was a thud as a jar of jam rolled onto the landing.

'My dear Bunter!' exclaimed Hurree Singh. 'You are a magician. You have turned a bottle of ink into a jar of plum jam.'

'Ow! Ouch! Didn't—came from Bunter Court,' gasped Bunter. 'You leave my jam alone, Smithy!' He dived for the jar at the same time as Vernon-Smith. There was a sharp crack of heads, and Smithy slipped onto the floor as Bunter reeled against the wall.

'Oh, crikey!' moaned the Bounder. 'That hurt.'

As the juniors clustered around Smithy, Bunter saw his chance. He grabbed the jar, and bounded down the stairs like a kangaroo.

Smithy staggered up, his face red with fury. 'I'll burst that fat fishcake all over Greyfriars!'

'Take it easy, Smithy,' said Harry Wharton.

The Bounder rushed off in pursuit, and Bob shook his head. 'My best boater. There'll be real trouble if they bump into the staff.'

Neither Smithy nor Bunter thought about that. Smithy just wanted to get his hands on the Owl, and the Owl only wanted to escape.

As Bunter careered down the corridor, he heard Smithy bounding down the stairs. He rushed along, his heart pounding and his eyes swivelling from side to side as he looked for a hiding place. He slid round the corner, the jar of jam still firmly grasped in his plump arms, and as he did so, a brilliant thought came into his head. Quelch was out!

It was dangerous to invade a beak's study, but Smithy, in his present mood, was even more dangerous. Bunter didn't hesitate. He flew for Quelch's study like a homing pigeon.

Smithy rounded the corner and caught a glimpse of the Owl slipping into the room. As he charged along the masters' corridor, Mr Prout, the fifth form master, opened the door of his study.

'What are you doing here, Vernon-Smith?' he asked, disapprovingly.

Smithy came to a halt and then backed away, livid at the thought that Bunter had found a safe refuge. Although he could do nothing about it right now, he wasn't going to let Bunter get away with it. He'd pounce on him later on, burst him all over the school, scrape him off the walls, and then do it all over again.

Meanwhile, Bunter breathed a sigh of relief as he

stood with his back to the door. Prout had got rid of Smithy for him. For the moment, he was safe.

'Tee, hee, hee!' he tittered. He would stay in Quelch's study for as long as he could. By the time he came out, Smithy might be in a better mood.

He knew that there was an element of danger in staying where he was. Suppose Quelch arrived and wanted to know what he was doing there. Billy Bunter turned the matter over, and then chuckled again. He'd say he'd come to ask a question about history. That should please the beast. But what should be ask? He sniggered again. He'd got it. He'd ask the beak if Magna Carta was signed in the reign of Edward II or Charles III.

Having solved that problem, he turned his attention to the jam. There it was, glowing ruby-red. He settled down in Quelch's armchair and, eyes gleaming, removed the lid. He liked food—any sort of food—but he loved jam, and this looked particularly good.

He looked round, hoping to see a spoon, but there wasn't one. 'Mean beast!' he mumbled, but then his eyes lit up as he noticed an ivory paper knife on Quelch's desk. He snatched it up, dug it into the jar, scooped out a wedge of jam and conveyed it to his mouth, and then he dug again. Chunk after chunk of delicious plum jam followed the downward path. Bunter was gloriously happy. He forgot Quelch and he forgot Smithy as he concentrated on transferring the jam from one container into another.

A little later, he was both surprised and disappointed to find the pot empty. Hopefully, he peered inside, and then a happy smile spread across his fat face. There was still a blob in the bottom of the jar. It was surprisingly difficult to capture, but Bunter wasn't to be defeated. He held the jar firmly between his plump knees and settled down to the task.

Chapter 4
Four Whacks For Bunter

While Billy Bunter was occupied with the jam, Mr Quelch was enjoying a stroll around the quad.

He stood beneath the shady elm trees, and sighed. He would have liked to have stayed there, but duty called, and Quelch wasn't one to shirk his duty. He had to mark the exercise books that were on his desk in his study, and so he adjusted his gown, took a last look round the sunny quad, and made his way indoors.

He strode down the masters' corridor, threw open his study door, and stood in the doorway, rooted to the spot, a look of outrage on his face. There, sitting in his armchair was Bunter, a look of intense concentration on his sticky face as he scraped away at a jam jar.

For a moment, Mr Quelch was lost for words, but the moment didn't last long. He took a deep breath. 'Bunter!' he thundered.

'Oh, crikey!' Bunter bounded out of chair, dropping the jam jar on the rug and the knife on the carpet. He stood blinking at his form master, his eyes almost popping out of his head with terror.

'What are you doing here?' rasped Quelch.

'Oh!' babbled Bunter. 'I—I came to ask a question about—about jam, sir. No, no, not jam—history. Nothing to do with jam. I—I wanted to know whether Smithy signed the Magna Carta—that is, Henry X or—or Charles IV——'

'How dare you enter my study? And where did that jam come from, you wretched boy? Did you take it from the kitchen? Mrs Kebble has complained about you more than once.'

'N—no, sir. I—I wouldn't help myself to jam from

'IT WAS A MISTAKE, SIR.'

the kit—kitchen, Mr Quelch. Never. This—this came in a parcel.'

'Indeed?' Mr Quelch didn't sound convinced.

'Yes, sir.'

Mr Quelch looked keenly at the fat Owl. 'And was it your parcel, Bunter?'

'What? Oh, yes, sir. That is, Gosling—that is, Smithy got it this morning—no, not him. Me.'

'I see. You purloined the jam from another boy's study and——'

'Oh, but it wasn't Smithy's,' stammered Bunter. 'It was a mistake, sir. If Smithy had any, it's in his study. I'm not here because Smithy chased me round the school while I hadn't hidden his jam under my blazer. I—I just wanted to know about Carta Magna—no, Cagna Marta——'

'That will do, Bunter,' said Mr Quelch, severely. 'You took that jam from Vernon-Smith.'

'No, no. Not me. I—it wasn't Smithy's. If—if Smithy had a bottle of ink, it wasn't in his study. He—he wasn't after me because I'd got apricot——'

'Be quiet, Bunter!'

'Oh, yes, sir. Thank you, sir. Can—can I go, sir?'

'You may not!'

'Oh, lor'!' groaned Bunter.

Mr Quelch regarded Bunter thoughtfully. 'I hardly know how to deal with you, you wretched boy. You are idle and you are obtuse. You are also the most untruthful and greedy boy that I have ever met. You have been punished time and time again for purloining food, but punishment appears to have no effect whatsoever.'

'No, sir. You're right, sir. Doesn't help. Don't make a scrap of difference,' agreed Bunter, hopefully.

'It is not so long ago that you took a pie from the kitchen——'

'It was a mistake,' groaned Bunter. 'I told you. I never went down to the kitchen. Wouldn't. Mrs

Kebble got it all wrong. She just thought that I'd gone down because she saw me coming up——'

'That is quite enough!' snapped Mr Quelch. 'I caned you after that episode, Bunter.'

'Yes,' said the Owl, quickly. 'Didn't do no good, though. Didn't help.'

'That is right. It didn't.' The Owl's hopes began to rise, but they were dashed as Mr Quelch went on, 'Perhaps that is because your punishment was not severe enough.'

'Oh, crumbs! Oh, lor'!' Bunter's face became even more dismal as he saw his form master reaching for his cane.

'I am punishing you, Bunter, for your greed, for your untruthfulness, for purloining food, and for your unauthorised entry into this room. So you see, there are four reasons for caning you.'

There were four whacks and four wild yells, and then the door of Quelch's study was opened.

'You may leave, and I advise you not to come back unless invited to do so by me.'

'Ow! Wow!' A dismal Owl rolled out, gingerly rubbing the seat of his trousers, and he wriggled his way sadly down the corridor and round the corner.

'Got you, you fat villain!' The Bounder pounced on his prey.

'Oh, crumbs! Ow!' wailed Bunter again.

The Bounder stared hard, and then let the fat Owl go. He gave a laugh. 'All right, you fat fool. You look as if you've had enough.'

'Yow, wow!' agreed Bunter, miserably, and he slowly made his way to his study.

Chapter 5

By Whose Hand?

'Hee, hee, hee!'

'Hallo, hallo, hallo! What's the joke, fat man?'

Billy Bunter didn't answer Bob, but he went on shaking with mirth, and his little eyes twinkled from behind his large, round specs.

The morning break was over, and the Remove had made their way indoors only to find the fat Owl already propping up the door of the form room. It wasn't like him to be early for anything except meals, but there he was, chuckling away.

'What have you been up to, my dear Bunter?' asked Hurree Singh.

'Who? Me? Oh, nothing. I wouldn't do nothing,' he said, with an air of innocence.

'Aha! So you have been doing something,' Hurree said.

'Eh? What?' Bunter sounded alarmed. 'It wasn't me.'

'What wasn't you?' asked Johnny Bull.

'Tee, hee, hee. Nothing. Don't you go asking me if Quelch is going to get a surprise. I wouldn't know. Haven't a clue. I don't know anything about it. Couldn't. I've been here most of the time, practically all through break, so if anyone got in through the window, it couldn't have been me, could it?'

'Ha, ha, ha!'

'You idiotic lump of blabber,' said Peter Todd. 'What did you do that for?'

'But I didn't!' snapped Bunter. 'Now don't you go saying I was, Toddy. If Quelch heard you, he might think it was me.'

'So what have you been up to?' asked Harry Wharton.

'Oh, nothing,' said the Owl casually, but his shoulders heaved with laughter.

'What were you in the form room for, you fat chump?' asked Bob.

'No!' hooted Bunter. 'Wasn't. The window wasn't left open, and even if it was, it wasn't me who climbed in.'

'You couldn't,' said Skinner. 'You couldn't heave your great carcass up to the window, not without help.'

'How do you know?' demanded Bunter. 'And it wasn't Dabney who gave me a bunk up.'

'Ha, ha, ha!'

'You frumptious fathead,' said Frank Nugent. 'You're crazy to risk more trouble with Quelch.'

'But I didn't!' yelled Bunter. 'Anyway, Quelch deserves whatever he gets. He whacked me for nothing. I couldn't sit down last night. Not that I've done anything during break. Couldn't. Wasn't near the window.'

Vernon-Smith strolled towards them. 'Whatever you did, guzzle guts, it was something to do with chalk.'

'Chalk!' Bunter started like a rabbit. 'How do you know? Haven't been anywhere near chalk.'

'You don't want him to know that you've been messing about with chalk?'

'Not likely. He might think that I'd written something on the blackboard. That suspicious beast——'

'Then why not wipe the evidence from your blazer,' suggested the Bounder.

Bunter cast a startled glance at it. 'Oh, crikey!' he exclaimed, seeing several smudges of white. 'Give me your handkerchief, Wharton, so I can rub it off.'

'Use your own,' replied Harry.

'What? And get it all chalky! Hurry up, Harry, old man. Quelch will be here in a minute.'

'Not likely.'

'Beast!' The fat Owl turned to Peter Todd. 'Lend me yours, Toddy.'

'No!' said Peter, firmly.

'Beast!' Reluctantly, Billy Bunter pulled out his own grubby handkerchief, dusted himself down, and shoved it back in his pocket, relieved to have got rid of the evidence.

'So what have you put on the blackboard?' asked Hazeldene, curiously.

'Nothing,' said Bunter, casually. 'Wouldn't do anything like that. Somebody else might have, though. I wouldn't know. After all, a lot of fellows think Quelch is a beast, don't they?' He began to chuckle again. 'Hee, hee, hee! It wasn't me, you know that, and you wouldn't split on a pal, would you?'

There was a burst of laughter, and Harry Wharton said, 'You're an ass, Bunter. If you've——'

'Tee, hee, hee. That rotten beast can think what he likes. He won't know who done it,' sniggered Bunter. 'I never signed my name. I'm not daft.' He shook with laughter. 'He won't half be mad. He'll know it was one of us, but he won't know who it is. I don't mind telling you,' he added, confidentially, 'that I'm fed up with Quelch. Do you know, he said that I was untruthful?'

'Never!' said Bob.

'He did,' asserted Bunter. 'It's insulting, that's what it is. We Bunters always tell the truth. When you come from an ancient line like mine, tradition is bred in you. That's why I never lie. Of course it's different for oiks like you, but we Bunters——'

'Sh!' hissed Bob. 'Henry's on his way.'

As Mr Quelch strode down the corridor, he gave the assembled members of his form a sharp glance before unlocking the form room door, and then he stood on one side, watched them enter the room, and followed them in, taking his place at his desk.

There was silence as the Remove sat down, but then the laughter began. It started as a small chuckle, but then it grew into a great roar. 'Ha, ha, ha!'

'Hee, hee, hee!' tittered Bunter, beaming all over his fat face. It was music to his ears—as good as applause. He realised that it wasn't going to bring a smile to Quelch's lips, but there was nothing that his form master could do. He'd never know who had written on the blackboard. Bunter gazed at the blackboard, proudly staring at his handiwork. It was a simple message:

QUELCH IS A BEEST!

As the gales of laughter became even greater, Quelch's brow became blacker. 'Silence!' he demanded, and then, realising that all eyes were directed towards the blackboard, he swung round to look at it.

The laughter died away as he turned back to the class, his face furious. His eyes narrowed as he looked at the Owl. 'Bunter!' he thundered.

'Oh, crikey!' gasped Bunter, in alarm. He couldn't imagine why Quelch had picked on him. How could he have guessed?

'This is your work, Bunter!'

'Eh? What? Not me, Mr Quelch. I—I don't think you're a beast, not like the others do, and even if I did, I wouldn't——'

'Be quiet, Bunter! I know perfectly well that you did this. It is quite, quite disgraceful. You must have entered the room during break. You came in through the window——'

'Oh, lor'! I never—that is, I never knew you were looking. I—I thought you were in your study when—when I didn't—Oh, lor'! Oh, bloaters!'

'I did not see you, Bunter.'

'Oh!' Bunter saw a ray of hope. 'Then—then it wasn't me, sir! I—I was in the tuckshop, that's where I was. Mrs Mimble handed me a jam tart at the very moment when I was writing on the blackboard—no, no. When I wasn't—that is, when I was buying a piece of chalk.'

Quelch breathed hard. 'I shall put you in detention this afternoon. You will stay here until the task that I shall set you is completed—throughout tea, if necessary.'

'What? No tea?' It was a fate worse than death. 'Wouldn't—wouldn't you rather cane me, sir?' asked Bunter, hopefully.

'Be quiet, Bunter!' said Quelch in an icy tone, and Bunter quaked into silence.

He sat throughout the rest of the lesson, a puzzled look on his fat face. For the life of him, he couldn't think what had led that beast to pick on him.

Chapter 6
Not Wanted

'Harry, old chap——' Bunter was in the doorway of the changing rooms.

Harry Wharton shook his head. 'Sorry.'

'Eh?' Bunter blinked in surprise. 'What are you sorry about?'

'Shortage of cash,' said Harry, briefly. 'Try Smithy.'

'If you think I want to borrow something—' Bunter said, with a great deal of dignity.

'No?'

'No!' roared Bunter.

'So why call me old chap?' asked Harry, and the fellows in the changing rooms grinned.

'Beast—no, no. Listen,' said Bunter, hastily. 'I'm in detention this afternoon. I bet that rotter Quelch has thought up something beastly for me to do. Just think, I'll be stuck indoors while you're outside playing cricket. Look here, Harry, you know we've always been pals——'

'Have we?'

'Oh, come on. Who stood by you when you came here? Who stood up for you when you were having a tough time?'

Harry grinned. 'Frank did.'

'There's gratitude for you,' said the Owl, bitterly. 'Fancy not remembering what I did.'

'But I do. You borrowed fifty pence from me the first time that we met. Come to think of it, you never paid me back. What about it?'

'Stop joking,' said Bunter, seriously. 'I was going to ask you a favour. You owe me one after all I've done for you. You see, I want to play cricket this afternoon instead of slogging away indoors. You know how keen I am——'

'None of us have any doubt about that, my dear Bunter,' said Hurree, gravely, and there was a burst of laughter.

'Keen enough when you want your lines done for you,' said Harry.

'That was yesterday,' said Bunter, quickly. 'I'm keen enough now. You've picked the team for the game against the fourth form this afternoon, have you?'

Harry raised an eyebrow. 'Considering we're playing on Little Side in about ten minutes, you suppose right.'

'But you can still make a change in the eleven,' said Bunter, eagerly. 'You're not much of a judge of form, are you? Still, you've probably got enough wit to leave out a dud and put a better man in his place.'

'And who's the better man?'

'Me,' said the Owl, simply. 'I'll help you out. If you go to Quelch and tell him how badly I'm needed for the match, he'll let me off. I'm keen, really keen,' he went on earnestly, 'so don't think it's because I want to go to Friardale this afternoon, because I don't. I just want to help you out.'

'It's nothing to do with Uncle Clegg's ices in Friardale, is it?' asked Frank.

'Course not! Mind you, I did hear he's got some chocolate peppermint ones coming this afternoon, but that's not what I'm on about. It's cricket. You can make room for me, Wharton. Leave out Cherry. He's not much good.'

'What's that? Who isn't?' roared Bob.

'You. You can't even hold the bat properly. I ought to give you some coaching.' He concentrated on Harry again. 'You could drop Toddy. He's pretty hopeless.'

'Am I?' Peter shot a look of loathing at the Owl.

'You could take out Hurree or Johnny Bull come to that. It wouldn't make much difference. And what about Smithy? I bet he doesn't want to play. He'd rather go off with some other rotters and smoke himself silly somewhere.'

As Smithy glowered, the rest of the team burst into laughter. 'The thing is, Harry,' said Bunter, confidentially, 'I don't care who you drop as long as you put me in. Just make Quelch realise how much you need me. He wouldn't want you to lose just because he'd put the best cricketer in detention——'

'Ha, ha, ha!'

'What are you cackling for? You all know how well I play.'

'That's right,' said Frank.

'There you are then,' said Bunter, complacently. 'I know why I don't get a chance, of course. It's jealousy, but facts are facts.' He began to sound bitter. 'If there was any justice, I'd be in the team. The trouble is, Wharton, you haven't got the guts to stand up to the rest of the oiks. But it really matters this afternoon. Drop anyone you like, old man, just so that I can go into Friardale—no, no, Little Side——'

'Roll away, old barrel,' said Harry, briefly. 'Joke's over.'

'What?' Bunter was astounded. 'Aren't you putting

me in the team?'

'Nope. Not until we've got a marbles match on.'

'Beast! No! I didn't mean that. Come on, Harry, help me out. Just have a word with Quelch for me. I'd tell him myself that I'm wanted in the team, but I don't think he'd believe me. Makes out that I tell lies. Say that I'm wanted——'

'But you're not.'

'I know. I'm too good. I'd show the rest of the team up. But that's not the point. The thing is, I must get off detention. Quelch won't know whether I'm playing or not, and even if he did, you could say that I'd been taken ill. How about that?'

Harry shook his head. 'Nope.'

'Beast!' shouted Bunter. 'Can't you get it into your head that I don't want to be stuck in detention. I'd even play cricket rather than——

'There's a good reason for putting him in the team,' said Bob.

Harry folded his arms. 'Now that you've finished——'

'But I haven't——'

'Oh, yes, you have. Johnny, just prod him with your bat, will you?'

'Yoo-hooop!' squawked Bunter, as Johnny's bat came into contact with his trousers. 'Whoops!'

He scuttled away, filled with indignation. It was true that he was more interested in Uncle Clegg's tuckshop in Friardale than in cricket, but he was hurt that he wasn't wanted in the team. Furthermore, he had fifty pence, borrowed from Lord Mauleverer, burning a hole in his pocket. Life wasn't fair. How could he be expected to go into detention when he'd got enough money to buy a couple of really delicious ices?

As the clock in the tower struck two, he made up his mind and wheeled his way towards the gates. As he passed Gosling's lodge, he eyed the porter uneasily,

wondering if Quelch had mentioned the fact that he
was supposed to be in detention, but Gosling took no
notice of him.

Just before stepping into the lane, Bunter hesitated.
He was hardly the brightest person in the world, but
even he realised that he was taking a chance. He'd
have to face Quelch at some time. Perhaps he could
say that he had lost his memory for a short space of
time, but would Quelch believe him? Sadly, the Owl
shook his head. Probably not. Quelch often didn't
believe him. He weighed things up. If he cut detention,
there would be trouble. If he didn't cut detention,
there would be no chocolate peppermint ice-creams.
There was doubt which was worse. He went out of the
gates and up the lane towards Friardale.

He might have made a different choice had he
known that Quelch, standing at the window in the
Remove form room, saw him as he rolled out of school.
Within a surprisingly short space of time, Henry
Samuel Quelch, equipped with hat and walking stick,
strode towards the gate, his long legs covering the
ground at a rapid pace. Although he didn't know it,
Bunter's prospects of ices at Uncle Clegg's were fast
fading.

Chapter 7
Mr Quelch to the Rescue

Billy Bunter was also covering the ground at a surprisingly fast rate. Ahead of him were ices at Friardale,
but behind him was Quelch and detention, and so he
hurried on, fearful that a prefect might be sent after
him.

'Hold on! Where do you think you're going?' said a sharp voice.

Startled, Bunter stopped and looked round. He had reached a spot where the branches of trees on either side of the winding lane met overhead. It was dim, and Bunter peered about, wondering where the voice had come from. There was no one to be seen, and so he stepped out again.

'You heard! Hold on!' It was a command.

'Oh!' gasped Bunter, for now he could see who it was. There, in front of him and leaning against a tree, was a man with a battered bowler jammed on top of his greasy, black hair. No one could call Billy Bunter clothes conscious, but even he thought that the ragged coat, the shapeless trousers, and the grubby blue and white spotted scarf were not actually the mark of a well-dressed man.

The man's chin was adorned by a three-days beard, and the rest of his face was seriously in need of a wash. His nose had a queer sideways twist to it as if it had had a hard knock at some time, and there was an unpleasant glint in his eyes.

'I thought I might come across a friend if I hung about here,' the man said, leering at the Owl and revealing yellow teeth.

Bunter backed away. He didn't want this short, burly man as his friend. He didn't care for those red-rimmed eyes and that broken nose.

'Stand still!' The man rubbed his hand over the stubble on his chin.

Billy Bunter took another step backwards, but the man followed him up. 'Hold on, that's what I said!' he repeated, sharply. A short, thick stick was tucked under an arm, and as he spoke, he let it slip down into his hand, and flourished it in the air. 'I'm a bit hard up, see!' he said, in a menacing way.

Bunter blinked at him in horror. 'Oh, I—I say. I—I haven't got any cash. My—my postal order didn't come and—and—and I'm in a bit of a hurry.'

'So am I!' The man tapped the cudgel in the palm of one hand. 'Heavy, this is,' he said, meaningly.

'Is—is it?' stammered Bunter.

'Want to feel it?' The man jabbed the stick in Bunter's chest.

'N—nun—nunno!'

'Then hand it over'

'Wh—what?'

'What you've got in your pockets—and make it quick!'

'But I—I—I say—Yooo-hooop!' roared Bunter, as Nosey Jenkins gave him a sharp tap on his fat head. 'Ow! Leggo! Help! Yarooh!'

As Nosey seized Bunter, he squinted up and down the winding lane, but he couldn't see very far in either direction. Although no one was in sight, he knew that he couldn't waste time. 'Come here, you!' he said fiercely, dragging the Owl onto the grass verge. 'I'll crack your head open soon as look at you.'

Nosey Jenkins hardly seemed to move, but Bunter found himself sprawling on his back while dirty hands went rapidly and expertly through his pockets.

'Ooooogh!' spluttered the fat Owl. 'Ow! Oh! Help!'

'Shut your mouth!' snarled Nosey, ferociously. 'If you make another squeak, it'll be your last.' A look of satisfaction appeared on his face as he found fifty pence in a pocket, but it was replaced by one of fury as he realised that there wasn't any more cash. He dragged Bunter about like a sack of potatoes as he ran his hands through the Owl's pockets yet again.

He was so busy that he failed to hear approaching footsteps as Mr Quelch rounded the bend in the lane, a grim look on his face. The grim look became grimmer still as he saw Bunter spluttering and sprawling on the grass while a rough-looking man rifled his pockets.

NOSEY JENKINS GAVE HIM A SHARP TAP ON HIS FAT HEAD.

As Quelch broke into a trot, his shoes echoed on the metalled road. Alarmed, Nosey Jenkins looked up, instantly grasping his cudgel, but he was too late. Quelch raised his walking stick and smashed it down so that the battered bowler resembled a pancake. Nosey yelled and clutched his head.

'You scoundrel!' Mr Quelch raised his stick again.

'S'welp me!' Nosey was on his feet in a flash, and he leaped backwards, but the second blow caught him on the side of the head. 'Ooooh!'

Mr Quelch followed up the attack, swinging his weapon from side to side. Nosey stretched out a hand and gripped the cudgel, but he dropped it as Quelch swiped him on the wrist.

'Ouch!' he yelled. He dodged the stick as it whipped through the air once more, and turned and ran for a clump of bushes. Quelch managed to get in one last blow, raising a cloud of dust from the back of Nosey's grimy coat before he wriggled away through the undergrowth, and raced off.

Mr Quelch watched him go, and then he returned to Billy Bunter who was sitting up, a fat hand clutching a fat brow. He gaped dizzily at his form master, almost more terrified of him than of Nosey. He tottered to his feet, eyeing Quelch with apprehension.

'Bunter!' Quelch's voice was like suppressed thunder.

'P—please, sir, I—I forgot——'

'Return to school immediately, Bunter!'

'Oh, sir! Yes, sir!'

The Owl trudged wearily back to Greyfriars. Uncle Clegg's ices had disappeared like a beautiful dream, and so had Mauly's fifty pence. All that was left for him was detention.

Mr Quelch remained silent, stalking along in icy disapproval, marched him through the gates, across the quad, and into the form room. He placed a piece of paper in front of the dispirited Owl, and stood over him.

Bunter quailed, anxiously eyeing the cane that lay on Quelch's desk, but to his surprise, it wasn't picked up.

Mr Quelch spoke at last. 'I shall have to consider how to deal with you, Bunter. I shall have to consider it very carefully indeed. I must warn you, however, that if you attempt to leave this room before completing this translation, I shall report you to Dr Locke.'

'Oh!' Bunter drooped. He'd have to do the beastly work.

'You do understand, Bunter?' asked Quelch.

'Oh, yes, sir,' groaned the Owl.

'Very well then.'

As Quelch strode from the room, Bunter groaned again. He hadn't the slightest idea of what Quelch was planning for him, but he did know that he was going to have do the rotten translation and that he wouldn't get it done before tea was over. It was the worst thing that had happened to him that day.

Chapter 8
Where is Bunter?

'Anybody seen Bunter?' Harry Wharton poked his head round the door of the Rag and looked around.

'What do you want that porker for?' asked Bob Cherry.

'I don't, but Quelch does,' replied Harry.

'Tried the tuckshop?' asked Frank Nugent. 'That's always a good bet. He might be there.'

'No, he isn't. I went there first.'

'Been in your own study?' asked the Bounder.

'No. Why?'

'Didn't you have a parcel from home?'

'He can't have got his thieving hands on that,' said

Harry. 'I hid it behind the armchair. Oh, well, I'll try the studies.'

As he ran upstairs, he bumped into Skinner. 'Seen Bunter?'

'Yep.'

'Oh, good. Where?'

Skinner grinned. 'In class this afternoon.'

'Clot!' said Harry, annoyed. It was bad enough having to waste his time looking for the fat man without having to put up with fools like Skinner. He tramped up to the Remove landing and then made his way to study no 7. He pushed open the door, and walked in.

'Oh, isn't Bunter here?'

Tom Dutton was alone in the study. Tom, who was partially deaf, didn't answer. He looked up. 'What do you want?'

'I asked if Bunter was here.'

'Hear? Of course I can hear. What do you want?'

'I'm looking for that idiotic fat Owl.'

'Who's foul?' asked Dutton, indignantly.

Harry tried again. 'I've got to find Bunter. Quelch wants him in his study.'

'How did he get muddy?' demanded Dutton.

'It's nothing to do with muddy. Listen, Tom. I've got to send Bunter to Quelch.'

Tom Dutton stared at Harry. 'You're round the bend. Bunter's not Welsh. They can sing. He can't. He sounds like a frog with a sore throat.'

Harry took a deep breath. 'Tom,' he said. 'Do you know where Bunter is?'

'No I don't, and I don't want to.'

Harry slammed the door, and went along to Lord Mauleverer's study. Since Mauly usually had a good supply of food, it was one of Billy Bunter's favourite ports of call. Mauly, stretched out on a comfortable settee, lifted an enquiring eyebrow as Harry's head came round the door.

'Seen anything of a blistering, blabbering idiot, Mauly?'

'Only you.'

'What?' said Harry, indignantly.

Mauly lifted his head. 'No offence, Harry, old chap. Just meant that I've seen no one but you.'

Harry banged the door shut, and looked up and down the Remove passage. A door opened, and Fisher T Fish looked out, and grinned at the sight of Harry's exasperated face.

'What's biting you?'

'Bunter!' said Harry, briefly. 'I've got to find him.'

'So why didn't you ask?'

Harry brightened up. 'Do you know where he is?'

'Yep!'

'Where?'

'He bolted up to the box room. Had a package tucked under one arm.'

'What!' Harry darted back to study no 1 and looked over the back of the armchair. His parcel had gone. 'That pilfering pelican!' He rushed back along the passage, raced up the stairs to the box room two at a time, and hurled himself at the door. It shook, but it didn't open. He pounded on the door, and heard a startled gasp.

'Bunter! You disgusting dustbin, let me in!'

'I—I'm not here,' squeaked the Owl.

'Open the door, you paunchy penguin!'

'Oh!' There was another squeak. 'I—I can't. I've—I've lost the key, that's what I've done. Anyway, old chap, it's not your cake. I'd let you in if I could, just so that you can see it's not your cake.'

'Oh, yeah? Then what happened to mine?'

'Did—did you have one? I—I didn't know. Didn't even know that you'd hidden it behind the armchair. I—I bet Nugent had it.'

'You lying hound!'

'No, no. Not Nugent. It was Smithy. Must have

been. He was hanging round your study when I wasn't waiting to go in.'

'I'll deal with you later, you guzzling grunter,' promised Harry. 'But you've got to come out. Quelch wants you.'

'Tee, hee, hee! Tee, hee, hee!'

'Come out, Bunter! I won't touch you. You've got to go to Quelch at once.'

'Hee, hee, hee!'

'Stop cackling like a demented chicken, you fool. There's nothing funny about it. Quelch looked pretty grim to me.'

'Pull the other one!' sneered Bunter. 'Can't you do better than that?'

'Listen. I'm telling you——'

'I'm—I'm not opening that door yet, Wharton. Haven't finished yet. No, that is, can't. The key's got lost—told you——'

Harry hammered on the door again. 'If you don't turn up soon, Quelch will be after you himself.'

'Hee, hee, hee!' tittered the Owl. 'Think I was born yesterday? You can't fool me.'

'Don't be such a clothhead!' shouted Harry, thumping at the door. 'I'm warning you. If you don't get down to Quelch in a minute, he'll come and look for you himself.'

'And so will the queen of the May!'

'Don't be an imbecile. He'll be on the warpath.'

'Hee, hee, hee!' As Bunter chuckled away, Harry stood on the landing, glaring at the locked door.

'Wharton!' There was a bark from the foot of the stairs, and Harry looked down to see a lean, angular figure staring up at him.

'Oh, golly!' He'd been right. Quelch's patience had worn thin and so he had come to look for the fat Owl himself.

'Is Bunter up there, Wharton?'

'I—er—I think——' Harry's voice died away.

'I see.' Quelch rustled up the stairs. 'Leave!' he said, and as Harry disappeared, he turned the door handle. When the door didn't open, he rapped at it.

'That you again, you silly ass?' squeaked Bunter, cheerfully. 'I've told you. I'm not unlocking that door. Can't. Won't. Anyway, the key's gone, and I haven't finished yet. And it's no good going on and on about that beast Quelch. He can go and eat coke for all I care. He's a beast, so there. Yah!'

'Bunter!' rumbled Quelch.

There was a moment of silence. 'Oh, pancakes!'

'Open this door immediately!'

'Oh, crumbs!'

There was a pattering of feet, and the key was turned in the lock. The door opened, and the fat Owl blinked out at his form master, his little, round eyes almost popping out of his head. In one fat hand was a thick wedge of cake, and round his mouth was a sticky rim of crumbs, and there was a pile of crumbs on the floor.

Mr Quelch's voice was quiet. 'Come to my study,' he said.

Bunter followed his form master down the stairs, his face expressing total dismay. He knew what it meant when Quelch spoke in quiet tone. It meant that a storm was about to break.

Chapter 9
Threat of Expulsion

As Bunter stood, quaking, Mr Quelch sat at his desk, his brow furrowed. Although he had not spoken for at least a minute, the fat Owl felt that each of those sixty seconds had lasted for the best part of an hour.

Billy Bunter was used to trouble. It was something that came his way every day, but he felt unusually uneasy as Quelch sat there, his gimlet eyes boring into him.

The Owl hadn't the slightest idea of why Quelch wanted to see him, but he had too many sins on his conscience to feel easy. He wouldn't have minded if Quelch had ticked him off and had given him lines, or had put him in detention again. He wouldn't have been surprised to see his form master flexing his cane, but the silence troubled him. He couldn't help thinking that that beast Quelch was going to be beastlier than ever.

A few more seconds ticked by, and then Quelch spoke. His voice was mild. 'Bunter,' he said, and the Owl wriggled uncomfortably. Why wasn't Quelch angry? It didn't seem right. 'I told you, Bunter, that I was going to consider the matter of your behaviour when you tried to avoid detention. I have done so.' Quelch paused.

'Th—thank you, sir. May I go, sir?'

Quelch didn't answer, but he continued to gaze thoughtfully at the Owl. 'I have come to the conclusion, Bunter, that you are wasting your time at Greyfriars. You are wasting both your time and mine.' Bunter's jaw dropped as Mr Quelch went on, 'You are lazy, undutiful, and slack—slack in class and slack on the playing field. You are not a credit to the school, and I doubt that you ever will be.'

Bunter was taken aback. He had had a vague idea that Quelch hadn't got a very high opinion of him, but this was a bombshell. 'Oh sir!' he said. 'Do you mean me?'

'I can excuse your stupidity,' Quelch continued. 'I can make allowances for that, but there is no excuse for your idleness, your inability to tell the truth, and your slackness. You are a disgrace to your form, and a disgrace to your school.'

'Me?' Bunter could hardly believe his ears. 'Not me, Mr Quelch. Perhaps you're mixing me up with someone else.'

'What!'

'Are you thinking of Wharton, sir, or is it Cherry or Nugent? It could be Toddy. He's not always——' His voice died away as Mr Quelch lifted up a hand.

'It is hardly your fault that you are the most obtuse boy in the form, but even so, you are capable of making a much greater effort than you do. Your idleness is beyond belief. Your preparation, if you do it at all, is appalling, and you are constantly inattentive in class. You have even,' and Mr Quelch's voice became even deeper, 'gone to sleep in class.'

'Oh, Mr Quelch, sir,' said Bunter quickly. 'I—I thought I had explained. I—I just listen better with my eyes shut.'

'Your untruthfulness is shocking, quite shocking.'

'But, sir——'

'There might be some excuse for your slackness in class if you were keen on games, but you are frequently punished for evading games practice. Only last week——'

'But—but I had a touch of—of plumbago, sir——'

'Your greed has led you to purloin food from the studies of other boys——'

'If you mean the jam, sir,' gabbled the Owl, 'it—it wasn't Smithy's, and—and that cake wasn't Wharton's——'

Quelch's frown deepened. 'Lines and detention seem to have no effect, nor do canings. You are incorrigible——'

'Oh, thank you, sir,' said Bunter, delighted to have something nice said about him at last.

'Your ignorance, Bunter, is abysmal. Incorrigible means that you are incapable of reformation, that you will never change.'

'Oh,' said Bunter, downcast once more.

Quelch eyed him steadily. 'I have come to the conclusion that Greyfriars is no place for a boy like you.'

Bunter jumped. His mouth fell open and his eyes

grew round behind his spectacles. The sack! Booted out of school! Expulsion! Quelch couldn't mean it, not just for cutting games and dodging detention, and for helping himself to grub and nodding off in class.

'Oh!' he gasped. 'Oh, I say! Crikey!'

'I have also received a letter from your father about your mid-term report.'

'Oh—oh! I—I hope it was a good one, sir!'

'It was not. It was extremely bad. Your father said that he was dissatisfied with both your conduct and your progress.'

Bunter breathed hard through his fat little nose. It wasn't his fault, was it? He hadn't written the beastly report. Quelch had, so Quelch ought to be the one to be blamed.

'Your father says that you appear to derive little benefit from Greyfriars, and I agree with him. I am inclined to advise him to take you away from school.' Quelch paused for a moment. 'I have no doubt that he will take my advice——'

'Oh, lor'!'

'However, Bunter, I am prepared to give you one last chance. Everything will depend upon your conduct during the rest of the term. If there is no improvement, your report at the end of term will be accompanied by a letter advising your father to take you away from Greyfriars!'

'B—b—but—' stuttered Bunter. 'I—I don't want to—to leave Greyfriars, sir. I—I—oh, crumbs!'

Mr Quelch looked at him gravely. 'The remedy is in your own hands, Bunter.'

Billy Bunter blinked back. He couldn't think what Quelch meant. How could he improve? There just wasn't any room for improvement.

'I hope that you will make the necessary effort, Bunter.'

'Oh! Yes, sir!' mumbled Bunter.

'If you are careful and attentive in class, and I hear

that you are pulling your weight on the playing fields, and that you have given up your despicable habit of purloining food, I shall be able to give you a good report. If not——' Quelch's voice took on a deep rumble. 'If not, Bunter, once you have left here at the end of term, you will not return again. The outcome depends entirely upon yourself. That is all. You may go.'

Billy Bunter almost tottered from the study.

Chapter 10
A Tale of Woe!

'Hallo, hallo, hallo!'

'Where's that cake, you greedy gudgeon!'

'Scalp him!'

'Skin him alive!'

As the Famous Five entered the Rag, they made for Billy Bunter and gathered round, looks of fury on their faces, but he seemed almost unaware of them as he sat in an armchair, his face gloomy and his eyes blinking dismally from behind his specs.

He had forgotten the episode in the box room, but the Famous Five hadn't. They had been looking forward to that cake, and they hadn't had as much as a crumb. There was no way that they could get it back—indeed, only an X-ray could have discovered it, but they could get their own back on the Owl. However, they paused. They had never seen him so woebegone before.

Clearly, he had no idea of the danger he was in. He just turned his eyes on them and blinked dolefully. 'Hallo,' he said, in a dispirited way.

'You plundering pelican!' began Johnny.

'Hold on,' said Harry. 'Quelch has been on the warpath. If he's had six of the best——'

'Did he whop you?' demanded Bob Cherry.

'Worse!' mumbled Bunter.

'Sent to the head?' asked Frank Nugent, and they all looked grave.

'No, worse than that!' groaned Bunter.

'You haven't been sacked, have you?' asked Harry.

'My hat!' Bob let out a long, low whistle.

Bunter gave them a gloomy look. 'Not quite, but it's nearly as bad. Same thing, really. I—I've got to leave at the end of term. I've got to go unless——'

'Unless what?' asked Frank.

'Unless Quelch does me justice for once, and that's not very likely. He's always got his knife into me. I—I say, you fellows, do you think Quelch is quite right in the head?'

'What?'

'He sounded as if he'd gone round the bend,' explained Bunter. 'You should have heard what he said to me. He said that I was idle, greedy, untruthful, and a slacker. Me! I can't understand it. If he'd been rabbiting away about one of you, that would have been different. But to say it of me—well, I ask you!'

'Don't,' said Johnny. 'You might get a reply!'

Bunter took no notice of him. 'He's never been fair,' he said, bitterly. 'Come to that, you haven't been fair either, Wharton. You've never done me justice. I've never played in a single match——'

'Ha, ha, ha!'

'I don't expect much from you, Wharton, but Quelch is different. He's a beak. He ought to put his prejudices behind him. He doesn't understand me. Slack at games! Huh!'

'But you are,' said Johnny, bluntly.

'Me?' Bunter gave him a contemptuous blink, and then went on. 'He'll give me a bad report, and he'll tell my father to take me away from school. It's fearful. I've been sitting here thinking about it. I don't want to go, and I'd be missed—no doubt about it.'

'There's too much of you, my dear Bunter, for there not to be a gap.'

'There you are then. And think of my young brother Sammy. He might go to the bad without me as his friend and guide.' The Famous Five stared. Bunter really was piling it on.

Bunter sighed again. 'Once before my father said that if I had to leave Greyfriars, he'd send me to some grotty state school.'

'What's wrong with state schools?' demanded Johnny fiercely.

Bunter gave him a disdainful blink. 'I'd have to mix with a lot of uncouth oafs, wouldn't I? Me! A Bunter!'

Johnny shook his clenched fist under Bunter's fat little nose. 'You jolly well know that I went——'

'Don't!' said Harry. 'He's got enough trouble.'

'I'm for it if I don't get a good report. I don't know what I'll do.'

'You could start working, you lazy lump,' said Johnny.

'And you could stop dodging games,' suggested Bob.

'Oh, really, Cherry!'

'What about doing your prep?' asked Frank. 'That would make a change.'

'And what about leaving other people's grub alone?'

'Oh, really, Wharton!'

'You could tell the truth, my fat friend.'

'That's a bit much, Singh!'

'You haven't got much choice,' said Bob. 'You'll have to pull up your socks or our Henry will do just what he said.'

'We'll be left wiping our tears,' added Frank. 'It'll be hard on us, won't it, Bob?'

'Tough,' said Bob, grinning.

'We'll have to get a move on,' said Harry, looking at his watch. 'Mauly's waiting for us.'

As they trampled out of the common room, Skinner, Snoop and Stott came in. They glanced at the gloomy Owl and, like the Famous Five, thought that they'd never seen him so down in the dumps.

'What's up, fat man?' asked Skinner. 'Been caught by Coker?'

'I—I say, you fellows. What do you think? I—I might have to leave Greyfriars. I might not be here next term.'

'Really?' said Skinner. 'What a bit of luck.'

'Sounds too good to be true,' remarked Stott.

'We'll put out the flags,' added Snoop.

'Beasts!' Bunter heaved himself out of the armchair, and rolled out of the Rag, leaving them laughing. As he made his way up the passage, he bumped into Squiff. 'I say, Squiff, old chap——'

'I'm broke,' said Squiff. 'Skint.'

'I—I don't want to borrow anything, Squiff. I—I say, it looks as if this is going to be my last term at Greyfriars. What'll you do without me?'

'Be a bit better off.'

'Oh, Squiff, not the remark of a gentleman.'

As Squiff moved off, Bunter saw Peter Todd coming his way. He hurried up to him. At least he could expect some sympathy from his study-mate. 'I say, Peter, old fellow——'

'It's no good. I've got no cash and I've got no food, and I've handed my work in so you can't copy it.'

'As if I would——'

'Good,' said Toddy, pushing past the fat Owl.

'Wait a minute.' Bunter grasped his arm. 'Toddy,' he said, dismally, 'I'm for it this time. How would you feel if you never saw me in study no 7 again?'

'Fine!' said Toddy, breezily.

As he marched on, Bunter glared at his back with concentrated fury. 'Beast!' he shouted, as he turned away. The fat Owl couldn't understand it. Here he was, in imminent danger of leaving Greyfriars, and nobody seemed to care.

Chapter 11
New Resolutions

'Smithy could open with Cherry,' murmured Harry Wharton to himself as he sat at the study table, a biro in his hand, and a sheet of paper in front of him. He was going through the cricket team he had selected for the match against Topham. It was an important game, and since the Topham side was a strong one, he was anxious to field as good a team as he could.

'Wharton, old chap——'

Harry didn't bother to turn round. 'Don't bother,' he said, briefly.

'But—but—Harry——'

'Buzz off, Bunter!'

'Oh dry up!' said Harry, impatiently.

The fat Owl did neither. Instead, he wheeled into study no 1, and shut the door. Several days had passed since he'd had that heart to heart with Quelch, and the cloud that loomed over his horizon hadn't lifted. If anything, it had become darker.

The fellows in the Remove hadn't been at all sympathetic, but he consoled himself with the thought that the full horror of life without him hadn't yet penetrated their thick heads.

What was more, as day followed day, he had become keener and keener on Greyfriars. Of course, the place had its drawbacks. Quelch didn't give him his due; the Remove didn't give him his due, but that, he decided, was because of jealousy.

He had made up his mind that he was going to stay at Greyfriars, but he wasn't sure how to manage it. Quelch wanted him to reform himself, but what was there to reform? Nothing! However, he had to satisfy Quelch somehow or other, and so he had decided to have a word with the captain of the Remove.

'I say, Wharton,' he said, reproachfully, 'you might be a bit more welcoming. You know I'm having a tough time. It's not sporting to put the boot in. I've put myself out for you more than once. I do think——'

'I'm busy, fat man, Roll off.'

'What are you doing? Quelch given you some lines?'

'No. I'm going through the batting order for the match against Topham next week.' He glanced up at the study clock. 'It'll soon be time to get down to the nets. Bowl off, barrel.'

'But that's what I want to talk to you about,' said Bunter, urgently. 'Cricket,' and then he added pathetically, 'You don't want me to leave the school, do dou, Harry?'

Harry laughed. 'I'll do my best to bear up,' he said. 'I might manage to get a piece of my own cake once you've gone.'

'Beast! Oh, I say, Harry, I didn't say that. What I meant was, I need your help, old man. You know the score. I've got to keep Quelch happy somehow. I'm jolly well going to see that I get a good report at the end of term.'

'Good for you. Best of luck. Now, skip, Bunter!'

'I'm going all out for it,' said Bunter, impressively. 'Shan't leave a stone unturned. I'm going to really get my head down. I'm going to mug up all that stupid Latin, and I'm going to learn all those French verbs. It won't take long,' he added, modestly. 'Not with my memory.'

'Oh, yes?'

'Yes!' said Bunter, firmly. 'I'm not going to some beastly state school. Look what it did to Bull.'

'Frank went to a primary school, and so did Toddy,' Harry pointed out, 'and——'

'I know. It shows, don't it? Well, I'm not going. It wouldn't suit my style.'

'And you probably wouldn't suit it,' said Harry, drily.

'So I'm going to get down to work.'

'That'll be a change. Now, clear off and tell someone else about it.'

'But I haven't finished,' said Bunter, eagerly. 'There's games. You can help me out. As you know, Quelch has got this idea that I'm a slacker when it comes to games. Well, I'm going to prove him wrong. He'll see that I'm as brilliant at games as I'm going to be in class.'

'Really?'

'Really! It's a pity you're not a sport, Wharton. You could do the decent thing and give me your job, but I don't expect you will.'

'That's right.'

'If we did have an election, I know who the chaps would vote for——'

Harry grinned. 'And so do I.'

'And so that's why you won't risk it. But still, you can help me out. All I want is a chance,' the Owl said. 'What I really want is a place in the team, and I want to play in a home match—Highcliffe or Carcroft. I'm not fussy. You can choose which you like,' he said, generously, 'but make it soon, will you?' As Harry threw back his head, and laughed loudly, Bunter blinked indignantly at him. 'What's that for?'

Harry wiped his eyes. 'You,' he said. 'Your little joke.'

'But I wasn't joking.'

'It sounds like a joke to me.' Harry looked at the clock again. 'Do push off, Bunter, and do your act elsewhere.'

Bunter snorted. 'Are you going to put me in the team or not?' he demanded.

'Not.'

'Oh, Wharton, you haven't understood. If I play well, Quelch will be pleased. It's time you got over your petty jealousy. You should play the best man——'

'You puffed up——'

Bunter swept on. 'And the sooner, the better. It won't half impress Quelch when he sees I'm in the team. It'll make him sit up——'

'Drop dead, I should think.'

'So what about putting me in the next home match?'

'No!'

'I expect he'd even come to see me play——'

Harry Wharton put down his biro, and turned to Bunter. 'Can't you get it into your fat head that we play to win. We don't do it just so that Quelch can have a good laugh.'

Bunter nearly burst with rage. 'You—you ass! I'm better than you, better than any of them. I'm not asking much. I've got to get on the right side of Quelch, haven't I? Anyway, your beastly matches don't matter. It's me staying on at Greyfriars that counts.'

'Oh, shove off, Bunter!'

'But——'

Harry Wharton sighed. 'I'll tell you what,' he said at last. 'Since you're so keen on cricket——'

'You know I am,' said Bunter, enthusiastically.

'If you get in some practice—a lot of it—I'll see how you shape.'

'Practice? I don't need any practice!' said the Owl, disdainfully.

'Oh, forget it.'

Bunter could see his chances of playing in the team

evaporating. 'I'd—I'd be down at the nets now, old chap, but I've got rather a nasty pain in my leg.'

'Which one.'

'I—I—I think it's the right leg. Yes, that's it. It's my right. It feels as if there's a burning dagger in it. I—I think it's a touch of plumbago. If it wasn't for that, I'd be having a knock by now. This wrist really is——'

'Oh, so you've got a bad wrist as well as a bad leg?'

'No, no. I can't think why I said that. It is my leg, honestly it is.'

Harry smiled. Bunter hadn't made much progress along the path of reform. 'You'll have to——'

He was interrupted as Bob Cherry, already dressed in flannels and carrying a bat under his arm, flung open the door. 'Time's getting on.'

'You're right.' Harry got up. 'Come along Bunter.'

Bunter gave a pathetic groan. 'I would, but it's this arm—leg, I mean. It's agony.'

'Don't be such a fool. It's compulsory. Wingate will find out, and he'll report you.'

'You're a beast, Wharton. You're the captain, aren't you? You can let me off if I'm ill—and that's what I am. It's like a red hot poker, this pain is. I'm as keen as mustard, you know that, but I'd just be a drag with pneumonia in my knee——'

'Gosh!' exclaimed Bob. 'That sounds bad.'

'Oh, it is, but I'll just have to put up with it,' said Bunter, bravely. 'I'm not the sort to make a fuss, but this is agony. I couldn't even manage the stairs. Come to that, I don't think I can get as far as the door. I'll just sit quietly in your armchair——'

'Not likely, you lazy lump!' said Harry.

'Don't be so hard on him, Harry,' said Bob. 'If he can't get out of the door, then he'll have to stay here. Maybe I should examine him.'

A look of alarm shot across the Owl's face. 'No, no. That's all right, Bob, old chap. I don't want to be any trouble.'

'It's no trouble at all,' said Bob. 'I think I'll just prod him with my bat, Harry, and see what his reactions are.'

'What!' roared Bunter. 'Keep that bat away, Cherry! Whoops!' He bounded out of the armchair as Bob lunged across the table.

'Well, well,' said Bob. 'He can jump. That's a good sign. Now I'd better see if he can walk.' He advanced on Bunter.

'Don't! I told you to keep that bat away!' howled Bunter, dodging round the table. 'Ouch! Beast! Stoppit! Stop jabbing me like that! Ow! I'm going!'

'Look at that,' said Bob, as Bunter fled. 'It says quite a lot for my treatment. He's sprinting!'

Chapter 12
Quelch is not Pleased

'Well, Bunter?'

'Oh, lor'!' breathed the Owl.

He really did want his end of term report to say that he was conscientious and painstaking, and he had intended to turn over a new leaf, but alas, the leaf had trembled rather than turned. His resolve had weakened, and he had continued in his old, happy ways so that he had skipped prep the previous evening, hoping that Quelch wouldn't ask him any questions about it.

His hopes were dashed. No sooner than the history lesson had begun than Quelch fired a question at him.

'Well, Bunter, I am waiting.'

'Crumpets!' Bunter flicked over the pages of his

history book, hoping to pick up a clue.

Quelch fixed him with his gimlet eye. 'Close that book, Bunter. I want to see what you know, not what the book says.'

'Y—yes, sir.'

Quelch folded his hands, and rested them on the desk. 'Then begin!'

'Oh—er—I—I've forgotten what you asked, Mr Quelch.'

'I asked you, Bunter,' said Quelch, patiently, 'to tell me what you know about the Commonwealth.'

Nervously, Bunter wiped his brow. Why hadn't he read that chapter last night? 'Well—er—' His voice trailed away.

Mr Quelch gave him a severe look. 'I trust, Bunter, that you did your preparation last night?'

'Oh, oh, yes, Mr Quelch. I—I did it straight away. Never sat down in the armchair once. Couldn't put the book down. Toddy had to drag me away from it.'

'In that case, you will now tell me what you remember about the Commonwealth.'

Billy Bunter's sluggish brain began to turn the matter over. He'd thought they were having a history lesson. Now it seemed to be geography, but Quelch didn't teach geography.

'I am still waiting!' snapped Quelch.

Billy Bunter gulped. There was nothing for it but to take the plunge. 'Well—er—it, that is, it all started with soldiers.'

'Yes?' Quelch sounded almost encouraging.

'And—and they fought their way to—to—to—well, all over the place.'

Mr Quelch put his finger tips together and leaned forward. 'You are not being precise, Bunter.'

'Oh—oh, aren't I? Well, to America and Australia and India and——'

'To America and Australia and India?' repeated Mr Quelch, astounded. 'Perhaps you will explain to me just what all this has to do with the Commonwealth.'

'I don't—I don't think that it was called the Commonwealth then, sir. It—it was something else.' He racked his brain, trying to remember its name.

'It was called something else? What are you talking about, Bunter?'

'I—I know, sir!' Bunter said, triumphantly. 'It—it was full of all these foreigners, Mr Quelch. All different colours, they were. All black and yellow and brown—black as the ace of spades, some of them, and they—they all rode on elephants——'

There was a gale of laughter as the Remove realised that Bunter was talking about the wrong Commonwealth. Not having done his prep, he had no idea that this was the name of the government in England after the death of Charles I.

'Silence!' rapped Mr Quelch. He turned his attention back to Bunter. 'You are a very stupid boy.'

'Oh, sir!' Bunter was dismayed. 'I—I thought —that is, I got it mixed up. Wasn't thinking——'

'Have you any conception of what the Commonwealth was?'

'Eh?' The Owl didn't understand the question. 'I—I mean——'

'Well?' Mr Quelch's patience was wearing thin. 'What was the Commonwealth, Bunter?'

Billy Bunter sat, a frown on his fat face. The Commonwealth? If it wasn't anything to do with the empire, then it had to be something else.

'Well?'

Suddenly, Billy Bunter's brow cleared. Now he'd got it, but it didn't seem to have much to do with history. It seemed more like maths to him.

'Its—it's like sharing,' he said at last. 'I mean, suppose Smithy has a cake, and Wharton has a pork pie, and Mauly has a box of chocs——'

'What?'

'Well,' said Bunter, eagerly. 'If they put them

altogether and then they asked me to tea, well, that would be it, wouldn't it? They'd supply all the wealth, and all of us would have it in common. Mind you, they'd probably be selfish beasts and keep it to themselves——'

Ha, ha, ha!' the gust of laughter became a gale.

'Be quiet!' Although Quelch was furious, it was some time before the members of the Remove could control themselves. Bunter stared round the class, affronted. For the life of him, he couldn't see what they were laughing about.

'Bunter! you are the most stupid and ignorant boy I have ever met. You are idle. You have lied to me. You did not do your prep last night. You will spend the mid-morning break in this classroom, and you will read the chapter you should have read last night, and you will spend this afternoon's half holiday writing an essay of not less than eight hundred words on the Commonwealth. If you have not completed the work by five o'clock, I shall report you to Dr Locke.'

'Oh! But——'

'Not another word, Bunter!'

Billy Bunter did remain silent, but he was filled with a sense of injustice. He'd done his best, hadn't he? It wasn't his fault if Quelch got history mixed up with geography, and geography with maths. 'Tain't fair,' he said, but he said it under his breath.

Chapter 13
Coker's Hamper

'Here! Give me a hand!' Coker wasn't asking for help. He was demanding it.

Bunter, plodding slowly upstairs, stopped and blinked down. The burly fifth former was dragging a very heavy hamper towards the stairs. Anyone else might have asked for help, but that was not Coker's way.

'Don't stand there like a stuffed dummy. Take one end of the hamper, you fool.'

'Oh, really, Coker!'

'You heard!'

Although others in the Remove would have told Coker to go and boil his head, Bunter didn't. He had plenty of weight to carry up the stairs without adding to his burden, but nevertheless, he turned back.

He went willingly. It was the hamper that did it. Coker was lucky enough to have a doting aunt, and if anyone knew how to pack a hamper, it was Coker's Aunt Judy. Nothing was too good for her favourite nephew, and so Bunter trundled down again.

Between them, they managed to heave the hamper up to the middle landing, and across it to the upper stairs. By the time they were half way up the flight, Bunter was spluttering for breath.

'I—I say, hang on a minute,' he gasped. 'I—I'm out of breath.'

'You would be!' snapped Coker. 'You fat, lazy, slack little porker——'

'Look here!'

'Stop yapping! Just get on with it,' ordered Coker. He humped his end of the hamper up a step.

'Beast!'

'What!' roared Coker.

'I mean—I mean all right Coker. Only too pleased to give you hand, old chap.'

Coker glowered at him. 'What was that you said? Did you call me old chap? I'll smack your cheeky head when we've got this upstairs, you tick.' He jerked his end of the hamper again.

'Ouch! You're pulling my arm out of its socket,' complained Bunter.

'So what? Now lift your end, you fat wart.'

Bunter breathed hard and he breathed deep, but he kept quiet. Within a few minutes they had got the hamper as far as the top landing. 'Give me a breather, Coker.'

'You should take more exercise, you fat freak,' said Coker, unsympathetically. He spotted Skinner making his way along the fifth form passage towards the stairs. 'Here you!' he commanded. 'Skinner, lend me a hand with this hamper.'

'I—I say, don't bother Skinner,' said Bunter, hastily. 'I—I don't mind. I'm glad to help you. It—it won't take long to get it into your study.'

'Shut up!' said Coker. 'Skinner's going to help. Come on, you twit! Take one end.'

Skinner walked on as if the fifth former didn't exist. Coker glared, and booted Skinner.

'Ouch!' Skinner tottered, but then he dodged past Coker and clattered down the stairs.

'I—I say, Coker, I'll help——'

'Then get on with it!'

They manhandled the hamper across the landing and into Coker's study. Bunter almost collapsed as he put his end down, but he rapidly recovered as Coker lifted the lid. There was a delicious smell, and Bunter's little blob of a nose twitched appreciatively. There was a glimpse of ripe, red apples and glowing pears. He looked at them longingly as Coker picked up a pear.

'Not bad,' said the fifth former, and then he put it

down again. He grinned at Bunter's disappointed expression, and then he gave a laugh. 'I bet you want to see what else I've got.'

'No, no. Nun—nunno. Not at all.'

'Then clear off.'

'Oh!'

As Bunter turned towards the door, Coker laughed again. 'Here you are fatty,' he said. 'I guess I can spare one.'

Bunter swung round, his eyes glittering from behind his specs. 'Thanks, Coker.'

'Catch!' Coker tossed the pear towards Bunter and grinned. He knew what was going to happen.

The Owl's arms shot up in an attempt to field it, but it landed with a bump on the tip of his blob of a nose. 'Ow! Ooh! Crumbs! That hurt!' he squawked.

Coker bellowed with laughter. 'Butter fingers! Now clear off and find Potter and Greene. Tell them to come here and help me unpack the hamper. I expect they're in the games study. Get your skates on, you fat flounder.'

Billy Bunter, still rubbing his injured nose, clutched the pear and ambled off. He made his way towards the end of the passage, passing the games study without bothering to find out if Potter and Greene were there. He wasn't going to deliver messages for Coker. The beast could take a running jump. He rolled round the corner and bit into the pear. It was just as delicious as it looked, and as he chewed, he reflected that he could dispose of a dozen more without any difficulty if only he could get his hands on them. He put his mind to work.

A little later, he began to chuckle. 'Tee, hee, hee!' He went back to Coker's study and poked his head around the door. 'I say, Coker!' he began.

Coker scowled. 'What do you want?'

'You're wanted, Coker, in the library,' he gasped. 'Potter's fallen down the steps——'

'Clumsy idiot!'

'But—but he's in awful pain, Coker. He—he might have broken——'

'Eh?' Coker sounded anxious.

'His neck——'

'What?'

'No, not his neck. His leg. He keeps on asking for you. I—I think it's pretty bad, poor old Greene.'

Coker stared. 'Who's broken his leg, Potter or Greene?'

'Did—did I say Potter? It wasn't him. It's Greene. He was groaning away and asking for you.'

'Clumsy clown!' Although Coker sounded unsympathetic, he rushed out of the room to see his friend.

Bunter watched the fifth former charge down the passage and heard him thundering down the stairs.

'Hee, hee, hee!' The fat Owl's hands delved into the hamper, and his little round eyes twinkled with excitement, but he had hardly started to examine the contents before two figures appeared in the doorway.

'You greedy gorilla!' Potter got in the first kick.

'You plundering poacher!' Greene got in the second.

'Yarooo!' An apple dropped from one fat paw and a pear from the other as Bunter bolted through the door.

Chapter 14
No Takers

'I say, you fellows!'

'Too late, fat man,' said Bob Cherry.

'Eh? what do you mean?'

. . . HE HAD HARDLY STARTED TO EXAMINE THE
CONTENTS . . .

'There's only half a sardine,' explained Bob.

'We left it especially for you, my dear Bunter,' said Hurree Singh. 'We thought that you might come fishing.'

'Fishing? Fishing for what?'

'For tea.'

'You're wrong then,' snorted Bunter. 'Mauly gave me tea. I just happened to drop in at the right moment, and so Mauly——'

'Couldn't get rid of you,' said Harry. 'Well, you can't be all that hungry after one of Mauly's teas.'

'It's just as well,' said Frank. 'We've only got that sardine.'

Billy Bunter looked indignant. 'I get fed up with you thinking that I'm only after grub. Well, I'm not,' he said as he stuffed the sardine into his mouth. 'I've got a lot on my mind. There's that beast Quelch. He's always picking on me.'

'Do you still think the Commonwealth means sharing food?'

'Stop hooting like that!' shouted Bunter, as they burst into laughter. 'It wasn't my fault. It was Quelch's. He shouldn't have made me think he was giving a maths lesson. The trouble with Quelch,' he went on, 'is that he isn't as bright as he ought to be, that's what I think.'

'Oh?'

'Not up to the mark,' said Bunter, confidentially. 'He probably realises that I've rumbled him and that's why he's got a down on me. It's not fair, but I'll have to grin and bear it.'

'And so must poor old Quelch,' said Johnny Bull. 'Fancy having to teach you.'

'He can't——'

'How right you are, fat man,' said Frank and the Famous Five laughed again.

'What are you laughing at?' demanded Bunter. 'I know as much as Quelch. More. I think it isn't worth trying any more when he says that the empire ruled Britain at the time of the Magna Carta. I jolly well know that Cromwell did it when he was sharing out the loot with Charles II in an oak tree.'

'Ha, ha, ha!'

'You can laugh,' said Bunter, 'but he knows that I know that he's pretty ignorant. I'm not going to waste my time listening to all that old rubbish.'

'Did you do that essay for him this afternoon?' asked Frank.

'Course I did,' said Bunter, virtuously. 'Didn't take long. I tossed it off. Took it straight along to his study. He'll be surprised when he sees it.'

'I bet he will,' said Bob Cherry.

'Still, I didn't come here to talk about that beast. I came about Coker——'

'Oh!' said Harry. 'What's he been up to? He kicked Skinner——'

'Cheek!' growled Johnny Bull. 'He's always booting Remove men. It's about time we took him down a peg or two.'

'Just what I was thinking,' declared Billy Bunter. 'That's why I came. Coker's got too big for his boots. I'm prepared to stand up to him. I've got the guts. The question is, have you?'

Bob grinned. 'What are you thinking of?'

'Coker's had a hamper——'

'So what?'

An eager look flashed across the fat Owl's face. 'It's not just any old hamper, you understand. It's from his Aunt Judy, and it's just standing there in his study. I dare say the greedy beast had some of it for tea, but he can't have done much more than pick at it.'

The Famous Five exchanged puzzled glances. 'What's the big idea?' asked Bob.

'Think of his face if it disappeared!' Bunter began to snigger. 'It would serve him right. So if you bagged it——'

'What?'

'Mind you, I can't help,' said Bunter quickly. 'It's not that I wouldn't. I'm not afraid of Coker, but I've got to think about Quelch. He's got this idea that I'm inclined to help myself to people's tuck.' He became indignant. 'He even thought that I'd had Smithy's jam the other day, just because I had it in his study——'

'How extraordinary,' remarked Hurree. 'I wonder what made him think that.'

'Dunno, but he's a suspicious beast. So if he hears that Coker's hamper's been looted, he might think it was me. You can see that I can't take part. All I can do is to mastermind the whole operation. Now, the first thing is to get Coker out of the way. Harry's got to go to his study and tell him that Prout wants to see him——'

'Oh, yes?' said Harry.

'Then, when he's gone, you can sneak in to his study and empty that hamper.'

'I want to get this straight,' said Johnny. 'You want us to pinch Coker's grub for you.'

'Not just for me, old man,' said Bunter. 'It's going to be equal whacks all round. Fair's fair. I'm not greedy. You know me too well for that. Now, once you've got it, all you've got to do is to bring it up to the box room where I'll be waiting. Now you do understand, don't you? Whatever happens, I've got to be kept in the clear. Tee, hee, hee! I wish I could be a fly on the wall when Coker opens his hamper and finds that there's nothing left.'

'You miserable microbe!' said Harry Wharton.

'You rotten robber!'

'You fat filcher!'

'Kick him!'

Bunter looked from one to the other. 'I—I say, I don't think you understand——'

'We understand only too well!' growled Johnny.

'But—but that hamper's crammed with goodies.

There are apples and pears and a cake. He's got peaches and cold chicken. There'll be plenty to go round——'

'You bloated bloodsucker, Bunter. Why should we want Coker's tuck?' demanded Bob Cherry.

'I—I hope you don't think that I was just thinking of tuck,' said Bunter, anxiously. 'I'm—I'm thinking of the way he's been treating Remove fellows. Wasn't thinking about grub. Wouldn't do that. I—I just thought it would teach him a lesson—more as a punishment than anything else. Teach him some tuck, you see.'

'Ha, ha, ha!'

'Blessed if I see what you're cackling for. It'll be as easy as pie. Coker will kick up a bit of a fuss, of course. He's like that. But if you all swear that you don't know anything about it, there's——'

'What!'

'If you all stick together, I don't see——'

'But I do.' Bob turned to the rest of the Famous Five. 'Didn't we hear Bunter say something about teaching Coker a lesson——'

'That's it, old man.'

'But I think we ought to get a bit of practice in first. Shall we teach Bunter a lesson?'

'What a good idea!' said Johnny Bull, enthusiastically.

They moved as one. The Owl gave an alarmed blink and turned tail, making for the door. Five feet helped him to reach it, and he disappeared with a roar, slamming the door behind him. A few moments later, a fat voice hooted through the keyhole, 'Yah! Rotters! Beasts!' and then there was the sound of rapidly departing footsteps.

Chapter 15
Stumped!

Smithy was alone in study no 4, comfortably seated in an armchair, a cigarette between his fingers, and the racing page of a newspaper on his knees.

There was a sound in the passage outside, and Smithy jumped as the door was opened. Hastily he stubbed out the cigarette and put the newspaper down. He would be in trouble if it was a master or a prefect.

He sighed with relief as a fat face adorned with a large pair of specs appeared round the corner of the door, and then he looked around for a cricket stump.

'You fat foozler!' he said, angrily. 'Haven't you been taught to knock at doors?'

'I'm in a bit of a hurry, Smithy,' explained Bunter. 'Those beasts might be after me. But it's all right—I didn't see you smoking. Wouldn't tell anyone anyway. I'm on to a good thing. Thought I'd like to share it with you.' He stopped talking as he saw Smithy's hand groping for something. 'What's wrong, Smithy? Looking for something?'

'Yes. Hand over that stump in that corner.'

'Eh?' blinked Bunter. 'What do you want if for?'

'You!'

'Oh, really, Smithy! I say, do listen. Look, I want to pay you back, old man.'

'You what?' Smithy was surprised.

'That's right,' declared Bunter. 'You've given me a good spread more than once, and I'm keen to do the same for you.'

'Come into some money, have you? One of your titled relations kicked the bucket, or has your postal order arrived? I've got an idea that you said something about one.'

'Well, not exactly,' confessed Bunter. 'I can't quite make it out. There's been some delay. The post isn't what it was. But still, that's neither here nor there. How would you feel about a little spread, Smithy? Nothing much. Just some cold chicken and jelly, and preserves and home-made jam, tarts and buns, apples and pears—a few trifles like that.'

'Got them in your trouser pocket?'

'Nunno! They're in a—a—hamper actually.'

'You mean that they're in Coker's hamper, don't you? I heard that he had one today.'

'The reason I came to you,' said Bunter, eagerly, 'is because you're not a coward like that lot in study no 1. You've got pluck—that's what I've always admired in you. It's your pluck, Smithy.'

'Oh, thanks.'

'Yes, you've got tons and tons of pluck,' Bunter went on. 'More pluck and more nerve than any other chap in Greyfriars.'

'Keep at it. Pile it on.'

'But I really mean it. I'm not buttering you up because I want you to raid Coker's study.' As Smithy began to laugh, Bunter looked annoyed. 'I don't know what you're carrying on like that for. I've always liked you, Smithy. I've never thought that you're a swank-ing fathead like the others do.'

'Really?'

'Really. That's why I came to you. You're different from Wharton and his gang. They're not plucky like you. No, if anyone's got the nerve to walk into Coker's study as if the place belonged to him, it's you.'

'Just hand over that stump, will you?'

'Never mind about that,' said the fat Owl, impatiently. 'I would help you, Smithy, really I would. That hamper's jolly heavy, I can tell you, but I can't give you a hand because of Quelch. I've got to get a good report, you see. I can't risk being caught. You mustn't mention my name, Smithy, if things go wrong. You see that?'

'Sure.'

'Now pin back your ears, Smithy, and listen. I've done all the thinking and the planning, so it can't go wrong. I don't want to boast, but I have got brains—more brains than the rest of you put together.'

'Of course,' agreed Smithy.

'What you've got to do is to hover around the fifth form passage. Then, when you see Coker and Potter and Greene go down for tea, you nip into their study——'

'Oh, yes?' said Smithy. 'I can see myself doing that.'

The Owl nodded in agreement. 'So can I. You'll find the hamper all right, but you won't be able to cart it away. I could have done it, but you haven't got the muscle power——'

'Holy smoke!' exclaimed the Bounder.

'Pity I can't help, but there it is. What you've got to do is to grab Coker's cricket bag and cram it with as much as you can. I don't suppose it will hold everything. You might have to leave some behind —anyway, it is Coker's grub. Then off you go. No one will see you, but even if they did, there's nothing suspicious about a cricket bag, is there?' The Owl was pleased with himself. 'It a pretty nifty wheeze, isn't it? All I needed was someone to do the donkey work.'

'Is that all?'

'That's the lot, old chap. It'll be as easy as falling off a form. Safe as houses. You get it to the box room, and we go halves. That crew in study no 1 said they wouldn't touch Coker's grub with a barge pole. It wasn't that. They hadn't got the nerve. I knew you'd be different.'

'Did you?'

Bunter missed the note of menace in Smithy's voice. 'I knew I could count on you. I don't mind admitting that I'd have been stumped without it.'

Vernon-Smith got up. 'I rather think you're going to be stumped after all,' he said, picking the cricket stump up from its corner.

'I—I say, Smithy, if you're going to be a beast—I say, keep that stump away!' roared Bunter. 'I say—yaroooooh!'

As the Bounder raised the stump again, Bunter bolted for the door. 'Ow—wow—ouch! Oh, crumbs! Oooooh!' His yells echoed up and down the passage for some time after he had left it.

Chapter 16

The Man with the Twisted Nose

'What a hill!' said Harry Wharton, dismounting from his bicycle.

'I need a breather,' puffed Frank Nugent.

'Me too.' Bob Cherry rested his machine against a tree.

Hurree Singh and Johnny Bull clambered off their bikes, and the five juniors sat on a log. Frank fumbled in his pocket. 'Have some,' he said, handing round a bag of toffees.

'I suppose we shouldn't have gone out of bounds,' said Harry, 'but it seemed a pity just to go as far as Courtfield bridge, and then turn round and go back again.'

'We ought to have got permission,' said Johnny Bull.

'But we didn't think of it,' Bob pointed out.

'Going into Redclyffe is against the rules,' said

Johnny. 'You know it is. And coming back through Redclyffe Woods is against the rules too.'

'We haven't done any harm, my dear Johnny,' said Hurree.

'We've broken the rules.'

'You needn't have come with us,' remarked Frank.

'Fathead!' replied Johnny. Of course he needn't have come, but the Famous Five always stuck together. If four of them wanted to ride back through the woods, then the fifth came as a matter of course.

'We're safe enough,' said Harry.

'Are we?' Bob had gone to his bike to get a bottle of lemonade from his saddle bag. He was staring up the leafy lane that wound up the hillside.

'What's up?' asked Harry.

'It's our Henry. I caught a glimpse of him over the top of the hedge. He's coming this way.'

'Are you sure?' Harry scrambled to his feet. All he could see was the top of a hat bobbing along.

'It's him all right,' said Bob, positively.

'We'll be nabbed,' said Frank.

'I told you we ought not to have broken bounds.'

'He'll come down on us like a ton of bricks.'

'He need not see us, my dear Frank,' said Hurree, calmly. 'All we have to do is to conceal our machines and ourselves.'

'Quick!' said Bob, and they wheeled their bikes up the bank, thrust them into a thick clump of bushes, and then dived for cover.

'Sure he didn't spot you, Bob?' asked Frank.

'Certain. Sh! He's coming.'

They heard the sound of approaching footsteps, and sighed with relief as they went past. Bob peered through the fronds of his bush, and saw the upright figure of Mr Quelch striding steadily down the lane. 'All clear,' he said, as he saw his form master disappear round a bend in the lane. 'Hang on a moment. Let's make sure that he doesn't turn back.'

'We wouldn't have had to skulk in the bushes if we hadn't broken bounds,' grumbled Johnny.

'I think we can come out,' Bob said, and they were on the point of emerging from the bushes when there was the sudden sound of running feet. 'Crikey! There's someone else in hurry.'

A man ran by. He looked very rough. His clothes were greasy. The coat was too large, and the trousers were shapeless. The blue spotted hankerchief tied round his neck needed washing, and his hat was a total wreck. A strong aroma of drink and tobacco wafted across to the juniors.

'I wouldn't like to meet him on a dark night,' murmured Harry.

'He is not a pretty sight,' agreed Hurree.

'What was he after?' asked Johnny. 'This is a lonely spot. We haven't met anyone else since we came into the woods. You don't think——'

'That he's after Quelch,' went on Harry, looking worried.

'He'd got a thumping great stick in his hand.'

Harry Wharton, followed by the others, pushed hurriedly out into the lane from the thickets. The man was still running and he could see, some way away Mr Quelch. The pursuer suddenly swerved onto the grass verge, and his footsteps could no longer be heard.

'See that!' exclaimed Johnny.

'He doesn't want our esteemed form master to hear him.'

'Could he be the guy who attacked Bunter in Friardale Lane?' asked Frank.

'Quelch handled him easily enough then,' pointed out Johnny.

'But this is different. Quelch took the bloke by surprise that time. Now the boot's on the other foot.'

The tall figure of their form master passed out of sight, and a moment later, the running man rounded the bend. Bob ran towards his bike. 'Quick!' he said, dragging his machine from the bushes. 'I could be wrong, but I reckon that Quelch could be in trouble.'

'Right!' The others made for their bicycles. By the time that they had reached them, Nosey Jenkins had already caught up with Mr Quelch.

'Gotcher!' he snarled, lashing out with his cudgel.

Mr Quelch half-turned at hearing a voice, but he had no chance of avoiding the cudgel as Nosey brought it down. Although it landed on the crown of his hat, the force of it made him stagger, and his walking stick fell to the ground.

Nosey Jenkins's red-rimmed eyes glittered. He hadn't forgotten the punishment he had received from Mr Quelch, and as the master reached for the stick, Nosey lashed out at him once again.

'Oh!' gasped Mr Quelch, and leaped backwards to avoid the blow. 'You—you scoundrel.'

Nosey looked viciously at him. 'That's right,' he growled. 'It's me. It's my turn now.'

In spite of his years, Mr Quelch was still very active, and had he been able to get his hands on his walking stick, he would have given as good as he got, but Nosey didn't give him a chance. All he could do was to try to dodge the savage storm of blows that rained down.

'I'll crack your nut open!' Gradually, Nosey forced Quelch backwards, and he gave a harsh laugh as Quelch stumbled. 'Got you!' There was a sudden shout, and Nosey looked round, his cudgel still raised high in the air.

'Watch out!' Bob shot down the hill towards the two men, and behind him came the other four juniors.

As Mr Quelch looked up thankfully, Nosey broke off the attack. With one bound he came into the hedgerow. He wriggled through a gap, and raced across a field to the safety of a nearby wood.

Bob screeched to a halt, fell from his bike, and ran

ALL HE COULD DO WAS TO DODGE THE SAVAGE STORM OF
BLOWS THAT RAINED DOWN.

towards the hedgerow, but he was too late. Nosey was already out of sight.

'Cherry, my dear boy!' said Mr Quelch, anxiously. 'Don't. It's a matter for the police.'

There was a clatter of metal as the other juniors arrived on the scene and let their machines fall onto the ground. They raced over to their form master.

'Are you all right, sir?'

'You look as if you've had a nasty knock——'

'You are right. That ruffian landed a blow or two— I rather think he might have bruised me.' Mr Quelch removed his battered hat, and regarded it with surprise. 'God bless my soul! It's ruined.' He put his hand to his head and felt it tenderly. 'Goodness! I really think my head is bruised.'

'There's a bump coming up on your head, sir.'

'And he's grazed your cheek.'

'My dear boys. Wharton—the rest of you—as you can imagine, I am grateful for your assistance, very grateful indeed.'

'We could ride to the other side of that wood,' suggested Harry. 'We might catch him.'

'It'll be a pleasure,' said Johnny, grimly.

'No, no. Certainly not,' said Mr Quelch, firmly. 'He is dangerous. As I said to Cherry, the police are the best people to deal with him. It was most fortunate that you were cycling in this direction——' His expression changed. 'Who gave you leave to go out of bounds?' he asked, sharply.

'Er—well, no one, Mr Quelch,' confessed Harry. 'We just did. We thought we'd cycle back a different way.'

'But you knew that you were breaking bounds?'

There was no point in denying it. 'Yes, Mr Quelch,' said Harry.

'Normally, I should take a very serious view of it, but since you have rendered me a valuable service, I think that I must overlook it.'

'Thank you,' murmured the juniors, realising that they weren't even going to be given a lecture.

'You will return to Greyfriars immediately.'

'Are you coming back, Mr Quelch?' asked Bob.

'Certainly not. I shall finish my walk.'

'Wouldn't you like us to go with you, Mr Quelch?' asked Johnny. 'We'd show him a thing or two if he turned up again.'

'No.' Mr Quelch shook his head. 'I assure you, Bull, that I really do not need a bodyguard. I think you have frightened the scoundrel off.'

Frank bent down and picked up the walking stick. 'Here you are, sir.'

'Thank you, my boy. Now go along—straight back to school.' He gave the juniors a nod of thanks, and strode off.

Chapter 17

Rough on Coker

'Yah!'

Bunter, seated in an armchair, jeered at the Famous Five as they entered the Rag. He was holding a peach in his hand. It was a large peach with a fine bloom on it, but surprisingly, he was nibbling instead of scoffing it. The slowness with which he was disposing of it suggested that even he had had enough. Clearly, he had been packing food in. There was jam around his mouth, crumbs at his feet, and apple cores in his lap.

'What's biting you?' asked Bob.

'We can see what he has been biting, my dear Bob. There are traces everywhere.'

'Yah!' said Bunter again. 'You don't know what you've been missing. Serves you right.'

'What have we missed? asked Harry.

'Ha!' said Bunter, mysteriously.

'Oh, well, don't tell us,' said Harry, turning away.

'I do not think that we have to be told,' said Hurree. 'I rather think that our fat friend has been disposing of the contents of Coker's hamper.'

'If you have, you must be mad,' said Frank.

Bob shook his head. 'You'll be for it!'

'Oh, I say,' protested Billy Bunter. 'You shouldn't say things like that, not even as a joke. I don't want anyone thinking that I've been anywhere near Coker's hamper. I wouldn't do that,' and stealthily, he slipped the remains of the peach into his pocket.

'What are you hiding?' asked Bob Cherry. 'It looks a bit like a peach to me.'

'Oh—oh, does it? It—it is one. It came from Bunter Court. My folks, they—they grow them, you know. Peaches and grapes and pineapples and figs and things. You should come and see our peacheries and figgeries one day.'

'Ha, ha, ha!'

'Don't you go round saying things about me,' said Bunter anxiously. 'Anyway, it's all your fault. If you'd backed me up, I wouldn't have had to go into his study—not that I did. You jolly well know that I've got to watch my step with Quelch. You funked it, and so did Smithy. He's just as much to blame.'

'There's bound to be a row. If you'd had the sense of a rabbit, you'd have kept well clear of the fifth form studies. Coker will raise the roof,' said Bob.

Vernon-Smith had strolled into the common room and was listening with interest. 'Correction,' he said. 'Coker's already raising the roof. He's carrying on about it in the games study. You can hear him from a mile off. He said that his hamper's been cleaned out.'

'Hasn't! Lying toad!' said Bunter, warmly. 'It's all

lies. I couldn't get everything into Toddy's cricket bag. I left quite a lot behind——' There was another burst of laughter, and he blinked at them indignantly. 'Not that I was there. Don't get me wrong. Didn't go near Coker's study, so don't you say I did. I don't want Quelch after me again. I say, Harry, old chap, if Coker happens to mention me, you'll put him straight, won't you? Tell him that I was out on a cycle ride with you.'

'But you weren't.'

'I know that, and you know that, but Coker don't. Anyway, I could have been. I like cycling. Can't get enough of it.' There was a burst of laughter. 'This isn't a laughing matter!' said Bunter, huffily. 'It matters to me. It's my future. Quelch kept saying I helped myself to other people's grub——'

'I wonder why,' murmured Hurree.

'Don't know. It beats me. Now, listen, you chaps. Get it into your heads that I didn't go near Coker's study. I wasn't there, and I never would have been if you hadn't backed out. So if anything's happened to Coker's hamper, I don't know anything about it. I never knew he had one. I expect he made it up.'

'Were there jam tarts in it?' asked Frank.

'No. Only a pot of jam——'

'Ha, ha, ha!'

'I—I mean—that is, I don't know what was in Coker's beastly hamper. I haven't had any jam, not for days and days.'

'In that case, you haven't washed for days and days, my dear Bunter,' observed Hurree Singh.

'Eh? What? What do you mean?' Bunter passed a fat hand across a large mouth. 'Oh, cripes! Am I sticky?' He dragged out a grimy handkerchief and rubbed his face. 'I—I say, have I got rid of it?'

The door of the Rag was pushed open, and Skinner bustled in. 'Is Bunter here?'

'Why?' asked the fat Owl, suspiciously. 'I—I might be. It depends. Who wants me? Is it Quelch?'

'No. He's still out. It's Coker who wants you. He'll probably be dropping in before long.'

'Oh!' Bunter's face fell. 'I—I—I say, Skinner. What's he like? I mean, is he in a temper?'

'You could put it like that. He was roaring and stamping all over the place.'

'Doughnuts!' Bunter got up. 'I—I say, if Coker comes here, don't say I'm here. I'll—I'll just get behind the door, and you can say that I've—I've gone to see Dr Locke.'

There was a burst of laughter as the fat Owl tiptoed across the common room and hid behind the open door.

'D—don't let on,' begged Bunter. 'Tell—tell him I've gone home—had to go to a funeral.'

'It'll be yours if he finds you,' said Bob, cheerfully.

'Sh!'

There was a heavy tread in the passage, and a burly figure appeared in the doorway, his face livid with rage. Coker glared around the room. 'Where's that snitching skunk Bunter!' he shouted, furiously. 'He's looted my hamper. I know it was him. Potter and Greene caught him at it earlier this afternoon. If I catch him, I'll spiflicate him!'

Bob turned round. 'He left you a message, Coker.'

Coker stared. 'What do you mean?'

'What I say. He's gone to see the head, and he's gone home for a funeral.'

'He can't have done both, you stupid tick!'

'That's right. You pays your money and you takes your choice.'

As the juniors laughed, Coker doubled his fists. 'Shut up! That's not funny! I didn't come here to listen to your idiotic jokes. I came for that worm Bunter. If he cleaned out my hamper, I'm going to burst him all over the school—and if he didn't, I'm jolly well going to find out who it was. If you give me any more of your lip, I'll smack your head, Cherry.

I've got a jolly good mind to smack it anyway.'

'What's that? You've got a jolly good mind?' said Bob, a note of surprise in his voice. 'You ought to use it now and again, Coker. We didn't know you'd got one.'

'You—you cheeky tick!' bawled Coker, his face red with fury. He'd been in a temper when he arrived. Now he had completely lost it. What he wanted to do was to smack Bunter's head, but since Bunter wasn't there, he'd make do with Bob's. He took one pace and lashed out with his hand. There was a smart crack. 'There! Take that, Cherry. I don't want any more of your cheek. Here! Let go! I'll thrash the lot of you. I'll—yaroop!'

He threshed about as a dozen of the juniors swarmed over him. Although he was big and powerful, he couldn't cope with them as they waded in. His arms, his legs, his ears, and even his nose was captured by the whooping crowd and, spluttering furiously, he was rushed to the doorway.

'Chuck him out! We'll teach him to come in here and throw his weight around!' shouted Bob.

'Urrgh! Leggo! I'll batter you! I'll—ow! Whooops!' He landed on the floor of the passage, completely winded, and the juniors roared with laughter.

'Coming back for more, Coker?'

'You'll be welcomed with open arms.'

'Ha, ha, ha!'

'I say, you fellows,' hissed the Owl from behind the door. 'Keep him out! Jump on him! Stamp on his head! Making out I had his hamper! Serves him right!'

Coker, still spluttering, scrambled up and dashed for the crowded doorway. Dozens of arms shot out and seized him, and he was whirled round and hurled back into the passage. There was a thud and a roar as he landed on the floor.

'What is the meaning of this!' Mr Prout rustled up

the corridor, his plump face flushed with anger. 'Whatever is going on?' There was a sudden silence, and the juniors moved back so that Coker was revealed. Mr Prout looked appalled. 'Coker! Have you been engaged in horse play with juniors? This is disgraceful behaviour—to think that a fifth former has nothing to do but to take part in rowdy games with juniors. You should be thoroughly ashamed of yourself.'

'Urrgh!' groaned Coker. 'I—I—urrgh!'

'Get up immediately!' snapped Mr Prout. 'Go to your study! You have no right to be here!'

'I—I—' Coker staggered to his feet.

'Go!' Mr Prout pointed a quivering finger towards the stairs, and Coker limped off.

Chapter 18
Report of a Raid

'This is a serious matter,' said Bob Cherry, gravely.

'Eh?'

'What is?'

'What are you on about, Bob?'

Faces turned towards him in surprise. The juniors had enjoyed that tussle with Coker, and because they were still feeling exhilerated, they were taken aback by Bob Cherry's earnest tone.

'What are you talking about?' asked Frank.

Bob folded his arms and looked round the Rag. 'I think it's a matter for the police.'

'What is?' asked Harry.

'You've only got to think about it.'

'Think about what?' asked Johnny.

'Coker's hamper. It's been looted. Nobody but Bunter would do a think like that, but——'

'Really, Cherry!' protested the fat Owl.

'But he's said that he didn't. Well, it wasn't him——'

'But it was!' snorted Johnny.

'That's going too far, Bull!' said Bunter, in a hurt voice. 'You ought to know whether you can take my word or not.'

'That's right. I do. You're as twisted as a corkscrew,' said Johnny, bluntly.

Bunter appealed to Bob Cherry. 'You believe me, don't you, old man? I mean, I swear I never——'

'There's no need to say more,' said Bob. He turned to the juniors. 'You've all heard him. He didn't touch it, that's what he said, and since we all know just how truthful he is——'

Harry frowned as he looked at Bob. 'What are you getting at? We all know that he looted——'

'But he's denied it, Harry.'

'That proves that he did it,' said Skinner. 'You always want to believe the opposite of what he says.'

'Beast!'

'You shouldn't be so hard, Skinner. We've got to take his word. What it boils down to is this. Bunter is innocent, and no one else would have done it, so it couldn't have been an inside job.'

'What the thump—?' began Frank.

'If it wasn't an inside job, then it must have been a daylight raid, and that's pretty serious. Although the thief only got away with the stuff from Coker's hamper this time, he might come back and see what else there is to lift. He might snaffle Bunter's gold watch——'

'Ha, ha, ha!'

'It's not funny. The thief must have been a pretty tricky customer since he didn't leave a clue. I know that Coker suspects Bunter——'

'Of course it was him!' yelled Johnny.

'He's denied it. He's sworn that it wasn't, and that means it has to be an outsider. I think we should report it to the police straight away.'

'Oh!' There was a horrified gasp from Bunter. He was delighted that suspicion had been diverted from him, but the idea of passing on the news to the local police terrified him.

'You must be joking!' said Johnny Bull.

'No, it's no joke, Johnny. What do you chaps think? We can hardly leave it until Quelch comes back. Shall I nip along to his study and ring the police?'

'I—I say, Bob, I wouldn't do that.' Bunter blinked around at the rest of the Remove. Their faces were grave. Bob Cherry seemed to have made quite an impression on them.

Harry nodded in agreement. 'I think you're right, Bob. He might still be in the neighbourhood.'

'He might even be in the grounds,' said Frank. 'I don't think we should waste time.'

'And since it wasn't Bunter——'

'And it couldn't have been anyone else——'

Vernon-Smith joined in. 'I don't think that we've got much option.'

A voice cam from the depths of an armchair. 'Yaas! Frightfully serious business,' said Mauly.

'Coker will be on the rampage again,' pointed out Toddy. 'We ought to get it cleared up before he tears poor old Bunter to pieces.'

'So you think that I'd better ring the police?' asked Bob.

'The sooner the better,' said Harry.

'But—but I say, you fellows——'

'I think you should get a move on,' said Harry.

'Righto. Leave it to me,' said Bob, striding from the Rag.

Bunter blinked around uncertainly. Was Bob really going to telephone the police? After all, ever since he had been at Greyfriars grub had disappeared, but it had never been reported to the police before.

'I—I say, it—it was only a joke, wasn't it? Bob has—hasn't actually gone to Quelch's study, has he?'

'A daylight raid's no joke,' said Squiff. 'The sooner they get their hands on the villain the better.'

'Rather!' said Frank, emphatically.

'Beasts!' Bunter looked anxiously at the juniors. 'He—he ain't going to ring the police station. He—he wouldn't do that, would he? Bob's—Bob's just pulling my leg, ain't he?'

'What an extraordinary thing to say, my dear Bunter. Why should he do that? After all, the burglary was nothing to do with you.'

Looking worried, the fat Owl left the Rag. Although he was almost certain that Bob was having him on, he thought that he'd better make sure. He rolled down the masters' passage, and stopped outside Quelch's door. It was partly open, and he could see that Bob was holding the receiver.

'Yes, officer,' he was saying. 'My name is Bob Cherry.' He paused. 'I am in the Remove at Greyfriars School. I want to report a theft.' Again he paused. 'The contents of a hamper have been taken some time this afternoon—a daylight raid.'

'Oh, pancakes!' squeaked Billy Bunter. It didn't occur to him that Bob hadn't actually dialled the number and that he was speaking to himself. 'I—I say, Bob——'

'What really worries us is the thought that the thief might still be in the neighbourhood. There are some valuable trophies here.' There was another pause. 'Thank you. Yes, we'll be waiting for the constable——'

'Stoppit, you beast!' squealed Bunter. 'Stoppit! Once they start nosing around—why, they might even think it was me, just like Coker does. I—I say, tell them it was a joke, old man. I'll—I'll share the stuff that's left with you.'

'Yes, officer,' said Bob.

'Stoppit!'

Bob turned round and put a finger to his lips. 'Sh! It's the police.'

Billy Bunter launched himself at Bob in an effort to grab the telephone, but Bob gave him a sharp dig in the ribs, and the fat Owl landed with a bump onto the carpet.

'Yes, of course. Our form master is out at the moment, but he will have returned by the time your man gets here,' Bob went on.

Bunter clambered to his feet. 'Stoppit, you beast! There ain't no burglar. You know there ain't.'

'Thank you very much.' As Bob was about to replace the receiver, the Owl, wild with anxiety, swiped him with a cushion. 'Ow! Ouch!' Bob staggered, and crashed into Mr Quelch's desk. Papers and books shot all over the place, and the old-fashioned inkpot shot off and fell into the fender.

'You—you twit!' Bob Cherry made for Bunter, and the fat Owl promptly backed into the doorway.

'Keep off, you beast! The beaks might hear us, and then we'll be in the soup.'

'You clumsy fool. Look what you've done. Look at that inkpot.'

'Blow the stupid inkpot,' hissed Bunter. 'You must be crackers, Cherry, getting the police here.'

Bob replaced the receiver, picked up the inkpot, wiped it off with a piece of blotting paper, and put it back on the desk. Then he straightened the books and the papers. He looked doubtfully at the fender. The inkpot had been full, and a large pool of ink was spreading all over the hearth. He shrugged. There was nothing he could do about that.

'Look—look here, you beast,' began Bunter. 'That is, look here, Bob, old man——'

'Shut up!' said Bob. 'We'd better skip if we don't want to be caught.'

Bunter followed him down the passage. 'But—but

what'll happen? Are they really going to send a copper?'

'You heard.'

When he returned to the Rag, Bob found a small crowd waiting for him.

'Did you actually pick up the phone?' asked Frank.

'Yes. Bunter got into a bit of a state when he heard me talking. I can't think why since he didn't know anything about it.'

'Ha, ha, ha!'

'Where is that fat ass?' asked Harry.

'He's on his way.'

'I take it you didn't actually dial,' said Snoop.

'Not likely. The only person who heard what I said was Bunter. It gave him an attack of the jimjams.'

'I wonder what he's got in place of a brain,' said Smithy. 'No one but an idiot would imagine that the fuzz would come roaring over because some food was missing.'

'Well,' said Bob, cheerfully, 'maybe it'll teach that pilfering porker a lesson. He'll be quivering with fear waiting for the police to turn up.'

'It'll dawn on him eventually——' began Harry.

'It will probably be dawn before he catches on,' remarked Frank.

'Sh! He's coming,' said Harry.

The door opened and Bunter scuttled in, a worried frown on his face. 'I say, d—d—do you think they'll actually send a copper?'

'It's their job,' said Harry. 'They'll have to.'

'But there wasn't a thief!' hooted Bunter. 'There wasn't!'

'So what happened to Coker's food? It's gone, hasn't it?'

'I—I say, suppose they think it was me,' mumbled Bunter, miserably. 'Would—would they run me in?'

'Don't worry, fat man,' said Harry consolingly. 'Dr Locke would bail you out,' and there was a burst of laughter.

'It ain't a laughing matter,' said the Owl, sternly. 'Not to me, it ain't,' For about the first time in his life he wished that he had resisted the temptation to help himself to someone else's grub.

Chapter 19
Bounder's Caught Out

Herbert Vernon-Smith strolled along the masters' passage, and loitered by the door of their common room. The door was shut, but he could hear voices inside.

Mr Prout's deep tones mingled with the high-pitched voice of Mr Capper, the fourth form master. He could hear the acid voice of Mr Hacker, the bleat of Twigg, and the mumble of Mr Wiggins, the dictator of the second year. Monsieur Charpentier was talking, and so was Mr Lascelles, the games master.

Smithy smiled. The coast was clear. The Bounder was about to drop in on Mr Quelch—at least, to drop into Quelch's study. His form master, as he well knew, was walking to Redclyffe. Well, if he was out on a long tramp, he wouldn't be returning yet.

Quietly, he padded down the corridor, opened the door of Quelch's study, and nipped inside. He grinned as he saw a pile of form papers on Quelch's desk. It was a large pile and he was quite sure that the moment Quelch came in, he would sit down and mark them.

Smithy had a good brain, and could turn in really good work when he chose, but he didn't always choose. He was well aware that the work he had handed in that morning was really poor, and that Quelch would take a very dim view of it, and so he had decided to remedy the situation.

He dipped his hand into his pocket, pulled out a tube of glue, and carefully pierced its stopper with a pin. His plan was very simple. He intended to stick each piece of paper to the next so that Quelch would find that he had only a solid wad in front of him. He'd know that one of the Remove had done it, but he wouldn't be able to pin it on anyone in particular.

He was preparing to spread the glue on the back of the first paper when he heard the sound of a car. He paused for a moment, listening carefully. There was the sound of footsteps in the passage. Smithy caught his breath. He knew that tread. Quelch was coming.

Swiftly, he screwed the cap on the tube and shoved it into his pocket, and then he moved away from the desk and stood staring at the bookcase. The door opened, and Mr Quelch walked in. He made for the telephone, and then halted as he saw the Bounder standing in the room.

'Vernon-Smith, what are you doing in my study?' He turned his gimlet eyes on the Bounder, determined to get at the truth. He knew Smithy too well to believe anything he might care to say. Quelch was already in a bad mood. His head was aching from the blow that Nosey had landed on it, so he wasn't inclined to put up with any nonsense.

The Bounder remained cool under his form master's keen scrutiny. 'I hope you don't mind, sir, but I wanted to look up something in your Greek dictionary.'

'Indeed?' said Quelch, drily.

He looked suspiciously at Vernon-Smith. Greek was not taught in the Remove. However, although Quelch didn't believe the Bounder, he was a fair man, and he decided to give Smithy a chance.

'Indeed! Then you didn't come here to play some

sort of stupid trick?'

The Bounder looked innocent. 'Oh, certainly not, Mr Quelch. I really was anxious to find out the meaning of a word.'

'What was it that you wanted to know?'

Really, Smithy was extraordinarily fortunate. He had come across some Greek a few days ago and, having a good memory, he remembered it. 'It was *asbestos gelos*. I read it only a little while ago, and I wasn't quite sure that I understood it.'

Quelch looked rather pleased. 'You must realise, Vernon-Smith, that it is not a word—it is a phrase. *Asbestos gelos* means inextinguishable laughter. It was used by Homer, and it referred to the laughter of the gods on Olympus when Vulcan was clumsy.'

'Thank you, Mr Quelch,' said Smithy, politely. 'That does make sense.'

Mr Quelch looked quite genial. 'Very well, Vernon-Smith. You may go.'

The Bounder swung round and made for the door, only grinning when his back was turned to Quelch. He felt rather pleased with himself, but then Quelch called him back. Puzzled, Smithy turned round. 'Yes, sir?'

'Come over here!' There was steel in Quelch's voice.

The Bounder walked over to Mr Quelch. 'What is it, sir?'

'You have lied to me, Vernon-Smith!' Quelch reached for his cane.

Smithy bit his lip. 'I haven't, sir.'

'You told me you come here to use my Greek dictionary. Is that right?'

'Yes, Mr Quelch. I told you what I wanted to look up.'

'You also told me that you had not come to carry out some practical joke.'

'Yes, I did, Mr Quelch.'

'Then how do you explain this?' said his form

master grimly, and he pointed a long finger towards the fireplace.

'Oh!' The Bounder looked in dismay at the pool of ink. 'I—I don't understand.'

'I think that I do. It is quite obvious that you have deliberately poured the contents of the inkpot into the fireplace.'

'But—but—I assure you, Mr Quelch, that I know nothing of this.' Although he protested his innocence, the Bounder could see that it was no use. Clearly, some idiot had been in Quelch's study before he had arrived, but Quelch wasn't going to believe him.

'There is nothing more to be said, Vernon-Smith. Had you merely played this childish trick, I should have given you lines or put you in detention, but you have lied, and that is something that I will not put up with.' He flexed the cane. 'I think it unnecessary to tell you what to do.'

'Yes, sir,' said Smithy, and he bent over.

Chapter 20
Beastly for Bunter

'Oh, cheesecake!' groaned the fat Owl. He had been sitting at the window of the Rag for over an hour, his eyes glued to the gates. He was uncertain, and he was anxious. Was a beastly policeman on his way or not?

As time had ticked by, he had gradually begun to feel a little more optimistic, but Bob had put on a good act and he still wasn't sure. There was a little crumb of comfort for him. At least he was safe from Coker. That beastly fifth former wouldn't return to the Rag for some time.

'Wotcher, Bunter!' said Bob cheerily, as he entered the room.

'Hoping to see one of the boys in blue?' asked Harry.

As other fellows came in, he gave them a dispirited blink. 'I—I say, Cherry,' he mumbled. 'I know you're just playing a rotten joke on me. Why don't you admit it? Come on, come clean.'

'Why don't you come clean?' demanded Johnny Bull.

'It would make a pleasant change,' said Hurree Singh.

'What's on your mind, fat man?' asked Bob. 'You haven't got anything to worry about. You're innocent. You said so.'

'Beast!'

'Cheer up, porker. Once they've got the right man, you won't have to worry about Coker—' said Frank.

'Rotter!'

'If you go on like that, Bunter,' remarked Bob, 'you'll make us think that you had something to do with it after all.'

'I hope you hadn't,' said Johnny. 'They'll get the man.'

'Oh, lor'!'

'Poor old Bunter,' said Frank, sadly. 'It won't help with that report if they do get their hands on you. Quelch will have to say that you were put in the nick.'

'Crikey!' gasped Bunter. 'No. That mustn't go in my report. My father—crumbs! It—it wasn't me. You know it wasn't. I—I was in the changing room. Wanted to get in a spot of cricket. Oiling my pads, that's what I was doing——'

'Ha, ha, ha!'

'Oh, oh! I—I didn't actually mean that. No, I wasn't there. Course I wasn't. I—I was in the tuck-shop, speaking to Mrs Mimble at the very moment when I was in Coker's study—no, no, not in the

changing room when I wasn't in the tuckshop. You—
you remember, Toddy. I was with you. Bought you a
jam tart from Mrs Mimble.'

'Think of another,' said Toddy. 'I'd have remembered. It would have been a red-letter day.'

Bunter looked hurt. 'Really, Toddy. If anyone
ought to stand by me, it's you. Still, I don't need an
alibi from you. Harry's going to let Quelch know that
I went out on my bike, aren't you, old chap?'

Harry shook his head. 'Sorry. I don't think I'd get
away with it.'

'But you would.'

'Nope. Quelch met us in Redclyffe Wood. He
couldn't have overlooked you. But what are you
worrying about? You didn't raid Coker's hamper.'

'Beast!' Billy Bunter turned back to the window,
and then he let out a startled yelp, and pressed his fat
little nose closer to the window. 'Oh! Oh, crumbs!
Crikey! Oh!'

Several of the fellows joined him at the window. 'My
Tuesday titfer!' exclaimed Bob.

Bunter stared at the police car that had stopped at
the lodge. 'He—he's here!'

'It's the law, all right,' remarked Frank.

'Yarooo!' Bunter cried. 'Oh, cripes! It's—it's me
he's after. I—I say, your fellows, don't let on that I'm
here. If—if I'm not here, he can't run me in, can he?
Never touched that beastly hamper. I—I haven't been
in all day. Say I've gone home— no, no, not that. Not
home. Don't want them calling on my father. Say—
say—oh, say anything, but don't let on that I'm
here.' He looked round wildly, and bolted from the
Rag.

He rushed along without the slightest idea of where
he was going. What he had to do, was to find a good
hiding place, somewhere, safe, somewhere that the
law wouldn't think of—what wouldn't they think of?

He paused and wiped the sweat from his fat brow,

and then an idea struck him. He made for the masters'
corridor. Quietly, he tiptoed along it and padded into
Quelch's study like a rabbit returning to its burrow.
Quelch was out. He was safe, he thought. He had no
idea that Quelch was in the masters' common room.
So, it was with relief that Bunter closed the door,
trying not to pant too hard.

His feeling of security soon evaporated. He heard
heavy footsteps accompanied by the clacking of high
heels.

'This way, Mr Rance.'

Billy Bunter, blinking with fear, put his hand to his
mouth. Mr Rance—the local constable!

As the footsteps approached the door, Bunter felt a
cold chill run down his back. Had he been seen
dodging into the study? As a tap sounded on the door,
Bunter took a quick step, and then dived into the
space beneath Quelch's desk. As the door opened,
Bunter held his breath.

'Oh, Mr Quelch isn't here,' said Mary, one of the
housemaids. 'I expect he's in the masters' common
room. You wait here while I go and see.'

The Owl's ears pricked up. Was Quelch back? As
Mr Rance entered and walked across to the window,
Bunter heard the sound of brisk footsteps. He almost
groaned aloud as Quelch entered his study.

'Do sit down, Mr Rance.'

'Thank you, sir.'

Quelch remained standing. 'It was good of you to
come so promptly.'

'Not at all, sir. We'll be delighted to get our hands
on the villain. He sounds a very nasty character.'
Bunter quivered at the determination in Mr Rance's
voice.

'I must admit, officer, that I shall be relieved when
you've taken him into custody. He's a dangerous
scoundrel.'

The Owl began to feel rather indignant. Was that

what Quelch really thought of him?

'I had a word with my inspector,' said the constable. 'I think we know him. He's an old offender. It
will help if you can give us an accurate description of
him.'

'I shall be pleased to do so. I assure you, Mr Rance,
that I am ready to charge him as soon as he has been
arrested.'

Bunter's mouth dropped open. He could hardly
believe his ears. Quelch was an even bigger beast than
he had imagined. He'd always known that his form
master had had a down on him—but to be charged by
him! It was ghastly thought.

As Quelch walked across to his desk, Mr Rance
took out his notebook and thumbed over the pages.
'Yes, sir?' he said.

Quelch stood, his striped trousers and well-polished
shoes clearly visible to Bunter. 'I think it would be
better, officer,' he said, 'if I jotted down a few notes,'
and he pulled out his chair.

Knowing what was going to happen, the Owl did
his best to screw his great bulk into a small a space as
possible, but it was a vain effort. As Quelch sat down,
his long legs came into contact with Bunter's stomach.
Bunter yelled, and Quelch leaped to his feet.

'Oooh!' yelped the Owl.

'Bless my soul!' exclaimed Quelch, equally astounded.

'What's going on?' Mr Rance bounded to his feet.

'I rather think——' Quelch peered beneath the
desk, and a fat, terrified face blinked up at him.

'Good gracious! Bunter! Come out! Come out
immediately!'

'I—I—oh, crikey! I—I——'

'At once!'

It wasn't that Billy Bunter wouldn't come out. He
couldn't. He was frozen with terror. Mr Rance was
there—he might be locked up.

'You heard me, Bunter!'

'I—I say, sir,' he babbled. 'It wasn't me. I—I never did it, sir, I—I was out of gates when I did it, and I——'

'Emerge!'

'I—I—I won't be put in the nick!' howled Bunter. 'I never done it. I'm not a villain, honestly I'm not. Don't let him lock me up. It's a mistake. Don't let him take me into custody. Oh, lor'! D—d—don't charge me, Mr Quelch.'

Mr Quelch looked despairingly at the constable. 'I'm sorry, Mr Rance, but I must get to the bottom of this. The boy sounds quite insane.'

He took a deep breath, reached for his cane, and brandished it at Bunter. 'For the last time, come out from under this desk!'

Although Bunter shook with terror, he didn't move. Quelch swooped, got hold of the Owl's collar, and dragged him out.

'Would you like a hand?' asked Mr Rance, approaching.

'Ow!' Bunter took one look at that blue uniform, scrambled to his feet and dodged round to the other side of the desk. 'K—keep him off!' he yelled. 'I won't let him put handcuffs on. I won't be locked up. I never done it. Couldn't. Wouldn't. It wasn't me. I didn't touch Coker's hamper.'

'You didn't touch Coker's hamper?' repeated Mr Quelch, bewildered.

'Yes, sir—no, no. No, sir!' gabbled the Owl. 'I never went to Coker's study. Not me. Wouldn't. Never knew he had it. It—it wasn't me who took a cricket bag to put it in. Never went near the box room afterwards. Didn't know there was a box room. I—I wouldn't do anything like that.'

'Bless my soul!' exclaimed Mr Quelch.

'It's—it's a mistake. Anyway, I won't do it again—not ever. But—but you can't let him lock me up.

QUELCH SWOOPED, GOT HOLD OF THE OWL'S COLLAR,
AND DRAGGED HIM OUT.

I—I expect Coker had eaten it all, and forgot about it. I—I bet that's what happened. I—I was in the tuck-shop talking to Mrs Mimble on my bicycle while I was oiling my bag.' As Mr Rance shifted from one foot to the other, Bunter turned a terrified eye on him, and yelped again, 'Keep him off, sir!'

Mr Quelch waggled his cane. 'You are the most stupid boy I have ever met, Bunter. Did you imagine that this officer came here to take you to the police station?'

Bunter's jaw dropped, he looked from Mr Quelch to Mr Rance and back again. 'Eh? What? But what about Coker's hamper?'

Mr Quelch looked at him in despair. 'Bunter—you foolish—' He shook his head and muttered, 'Grant me patience!'

'But—but, that is, I—I thought, that is, you—you said that I'd be locked up. You said that—that you were going to charge me.'

Mr Rance turned away to hide his smile as Mr Quelch said, 'This police officer came here to take down a description of the man who assaulted me in Redclyffe Wood this afternoon.'

'Not—not about Coker's hamper? But—but Cherry said——'

'That will do!' snapped Quelch. 'Obviously, you have been helping yourself to other people's food. Leave my study. I shall deal with you later.'

'Oh, Mr Quelch! I never—not me. Wouldn't——'

As Quelch brandished his cane once more, Bunter scuttled from the room. He realised that the sooner he went, the better. Mr Rance was no longer dangerous, but his form master was. He had the look of a lion about to pounce on his prey.

Miserably, the Owl returned to the Rag. There was a burst of laughter as he went in. 'Hallo, hallo, hallo! Hasn't he run you in yet, fat man?'

'Beast!' Bunter shook a podgy fist at Bob Cherry.

'Beast! I say, he—he didn't come about Coker's hamper at all—I—I hid in Quelch's study for nothing, and then he found me under the desk. Crikey! He wasn't half mad——'

'Surely not, my dear Bunter.'

'He was. He was livid, and he said he was going to send for me later. Oh, lor'! He was just like a wild beast. He was in a terrible rage. I bet he'll give me——'

'Six of the best!' chorused the juniors, and they were right.

Chapter 21
The Big Idea

'Prep!' said Peter Todd.

'Yah!'

Toddy and Tom Dutton were sitting at their study table, their books open. Billy Bunter was in the armchair, a glum expression on his fat face.

'You'd better start, Bunter,' warned Toddy. 'Quelch will probably want to hear your translation in the morning.'

'Blow Quelch!'

'Don't be an ass. Unless you get down to work, you won't get a good report.'

Bunter curled his fat lip. 'What's the point of working?' he said, bitterly. 'It's a waste of time. You know what Quelch thinks of me. He said I was slack at games and slack at work. Well, I showed him I wasn't slack at work. Gave him the right answer first time, and then what happened? Got a detention—lost a half holiday, and all because I thought he was giving a geography lesson—or maths.'

'But he doesn't teach maths and geography,' Toddy pointed out.

'I know that. He doesn't teach them because he don't know anything about them.' The fat Owl became even gloomier. 'It's a bit much when even my friends won't help me out. I asked Wharton to put me in the team so that I could show Quelch what a good cricketer I was, and he turned me down. Nobody gives me a chance. Do you know, Toddy, if my father would send me to Eton or Harrow, I'd clear out of Greyfriars tomorrow. I'd soon make my mark there, I can tell you.'

'Tough on Eton and Harrow,' said Toddy. They don't know what they're missing.'

'That's what I think,' declared Bunter. 'And Quelch won't know what he's missed until I've gone. He'll have lost about the only fellow in the class who's likely to be a credit to him. Later on, when I'm rich and famous——'

'Oh, yes?'

'As I was saying, when I'm rich and famous, and Bunter has become a household name, he'll realise what a mistake he made. He could have shared in my glory, and gone down in history books as the man who had taught me.'

'Very likely,' said Toddy, gravely.

'But still, since my father won't send me to Eton or Harrow, I'm jolly well going to stop here. I'm not going to some beastly state school. Mind you, I bet it would be proud to have me. I'd be top of the class, captain of footer and cricket—it wouldn't take long. But still I'm not going to one, so that's that. I'm staying here.'

'Then give your jaw a rest, fathead. Get on with your prep.'

'Blow prep! I've got something more important to

think about,' said Bunter irritably. 'Now that Quelch knows about Coker's hamper, he's got it into his head that it was something to do with me. I wouldn't mind if he'd only let the matter drop, but he won't. He made out that I'd helped myself. Me!' Bunter looked really offended.

'Well?'

'And do you know what that beast said? He said I'd got to return it all to Coker, and that if I didn't, I'd got to pay for it. How can I return it when it's all gone—not that I know anything about it. Coker's a beast, but he's not as beastly as Quelch. He'd have just thumped me—no, no, not me. He'd have thumped whoever it was with a cricket stump. He's not sordid, not like Quelch. It's sordid, talking about money. He ain't a gentleman.' Bunter gave a scornful sniff. 'I can't think where he was brought up.'

Toddy kept a straight face. 'It's disgusting,' he said.

'Yes, that's the word—disgusting,' agreed Bunter. 'You haven't usually got much upstairs, Toddy, but you've hit the nail on the head this time. So, just because Quelch is sordid and disgusting, I've got to raise ten quid. I've got to hand a tenner to Quelch so that he can give it to Coker. I jolly well know what Coker would have rather whacked someone, but Quelch wouldn't go along with that. He's—he's——'

'Sordid?'

'Sordid. Honestly, I was on the point of throwing a tenner on his desk—just like that,' said Bunter, making a gesture.

'And why didn't you?' asked Toddy.

'I hadn't got one,' confessed Bunter. 'I'd have had it right enough, if my postal order had turned up. I think I told you that there was one on the way, didn't I, Toddy, old chap?'

'I do believe you mentioned it once or twice.'

Bunter sighed. 'But there you are. It didn't come. To tell you the truth, Toddy, I'm stoney broke. Skint.

It's a bit awkward. I' don't suppose you could help me out, could you?'

'Back to prep,' said Toddy, briskly.

'I'm not talking about prep,' complained Bunter. 'I'm talking about cash. What about it, Toddy?'

'Not a hope,' said Toddy. 'I'm skint.'

'Well, it's got to be paid,' said Bunter, morosely. 'Quelch made that quite clear. I'd be willing to let the matter drop. I don't like talking about money. It's beneath me. The trouble is Quelch. He's no gentleman. It was the same once before when I ran up a bit of an account at the tuckshop. Quelch——'

Peter turned back to his books. 'Shut up, Bunter. Get down to some work.'

'Forget that rot, Toddy. This is more important than prep. I've got to get hold of that money. If I don't, Quelch's going to write to my father, and there won't half be a row. What I want is a good report. I don't want him writing begging letters to my father.'

'Get on with your Latin.'

'Latin! I can't waste my time doing Latin. Just think, Toddy. I've got to lower myself, just for Quelch. I've got to get my hands on some cash. I say, Toddy, I'm really counting on my pals to help me out.'

'Are you?'

Bunter shook his head sadly. 'Do you know, one of them's let me down already. I went up to Mauly's, and do you know what he did? He banged the door— jolly nearly banged it on my nose. Mauly's becoming stingy, that's what he is. I'm glad you're not like that, Toddy. I'll pay you back out of my postal order.'

'Hard luck, Bunter. I told you I'm skint. All I've got is about twenty pence.'

'Oh! It must be rotten to be poor,' said the fat Owl, sympathetically. 'One of these days, Toddy, I'll take you to Bunter Court so you can have some idea of how the rich live. Give you a taste of wealth and luxury.' As Peter laughed, he went on, 'Only too pleased to give you a spot of pleasure, old man. Now, about that money. What am I to do?'

'I've got it!' said Toddy.

'Oh?' Bunter's face lit up.

'Ask Quelch if you can use his phone. Ring Bunter Court——'

'Eh?

'And hey presto! You'll be in the money. They won't miss a few quid, not with all that wealth and luxury around.'

'Really, Toddy!'

'And now shut up. I've got some work to do, and if you'd got any sense, you'd do some too.'

'Beast!' As Toddy settled down again, Bunter thought about his problem. Somehow he had to solve it. He sat thinking, and then, quite suddenly, he beamed 'Tee, hee, hee!' he chuckled. 'I've got it!'

Peter glanced round. 'Come up with a solution?'

'Tee, hee, hee! I think so.'

'And who's going to be the victim?'

'I wouldn't borrow money,' said Bunter.

'No?'

'No! It would be difficult to borrow ten quid—not that I would, but there's hardly anybody who's got that much. Actually, I wouldn't lower myself to raise the money that way. I dare say you could, Toddy, but then, we don't come from the same background, do we? No. I've come up with a really good wheeze. What about a fund?'

'A fund?'

'That's right—a fund. There's nearly thirty fellows in the form. Ten quid is a thousand pence, ain't it?' He frowned as he began to work it out. 'Thirty into ten won't go. Thirty into a hundred goes two and forty over. Thirty in four hundred goes ten and ten over—' He scratched his head. 'Where had I got to?'

'Thirty into a hundred goes three,' said Toddy, patiently.

'That's what I said!' snapped Bunter. 'Three and twenty over——'

'Ten,' said Toddy.

'What? are you sure?' Bunter began to work it out on his fingers. 'Pretend three into ten. That goes three, and one over.' He glared at Toddy. 'It's one over, you fool. Thirty into ten won't go. Oh, that can't be right. They've got to give me more than ten pence each.' He pondered. 'Thirty times ten makes—what does it make, Toddy?'

Toddy looked up again. 'It's just over thirty-three pence each, blockhead.'

'Thirty-three pence? Are you sure?'

'Oh, shut up, Bunter,' said Toddy, wearily. 'Work it out for yourself.'

'Some will be more generous than others, I dare say,' went on Bunter. 'Mind you, I'll let them donate just what they like. I shan't make rules.'

'That's good of you,' said Peter, sarcastically.

'I know,' said Bunter, complacently. 'That's because I'm decent. That's what'll make chaps fall over themselves to help me. You should take a leaf out of my book, Toddy. Be decent, play the game, be generous and thoughtful.' He paused. 'What are you grinning at?'

'Nothing. Nothing at all. You get on with it, Bunter.'

'I'll have a word with the chaps in the Rag. No. No, on second thoughts I'll put a notice on the wall. It'll be a bit more official. Move over, Toddy. Make a bit of room at the table.'

'There's still time to do a spot of prep.'

'Prep!' Bunter looked at Toddy, astounded. 'You must be mad. I've got real work to do!'

Chapter 22
The Fund

'Hold on, you chaps!'

'What for?'

'Look at that before you go down.' Proudly, Bunter waved a fat hand at a sheet of paper pinned to the wall of the landing. The moment the bell had rung to mark the end of prep, he had rushed from his study to put it up, and he had remained there so that he could point it out before the fellows went down to the Rag.

Skinner, Snoop and Stott were first. They went over to the notice, and then gave a yell of laughter.

Bunter blinked reproachfully at them. He couldn't see what they were laughing at. 'I say,' he said earnestly. 'It's not a joke. Why—why don't you just trot along to my study now? Not that I expect much from you, Skinner. Everyone knows how stingy you are, but you ought to do your bit.'

Vernon-Smith and Redwing appeared. Skinner saved Bunter the trouble of pointing out the notice. 'Here!' he shouted. 'Come and look at this!'

The Bounder and Tom Redwing wandered across, and then, like the others, they burst into laughter.

'Hallo, hallo, hallo! What's the joke?' asked Bob Cherry.

The Famous Five halted, read the notice, and hooted with laughter.

'What are you lot cackling for?' demanded Bunter, crossly, and he became more and more annoyed as the crowd grew and the hilarity became greater. He had wondered at first if anybody would bother to read his notice, but he need not have worried. They couldn't tear themselves away from it.

NOTISE
THE BUNTER PHUND
All my pals in the Remove are hearby
rekwested to rally rouwnd and help a
chap out of a hole.
THE WEEKS GOOD CORSE!
Every fellow willing to help a pal
out of a bad phix, please step into
study no 7 and put something in the
box on the tabel. Small contributions
thankfuly receeved. Shell out your
quids and your coines.
Singed
W. G. Bunter
PS Nuthing refewsed no mater how small

The fat Owl felt offended at the reception of his notice.
He had put much more effort into it than he ever had
done into prep, and he flattered himself that he had
worded it rather well. He'd thought it might create
some interest, but the attention it was getting wasn't
what he'd expected. Fellows were falling about with
laughter.

'There's your chance, Mauly!' shouted Bob. 'Don't
forget to shove in a quid or two. And what about you,
Smithy? You can get rid of some of your filthy lucre.'

'That sure takes the cake!' observed Fisher T Fish.
'That's the elephant's hind leg! It sure is the grass-
hopper's whiskers!'

'Cough up your dollars and dimes, Fishy!' laughed
Frank.

Bunter brightened up. 'I knew I could count on you
lot,' he squeaked excitedly. 'I knew you wouldn't let
me down. I've got to give Quelch ten quid to pay for
the stuff out of Coker's hamper. Not that I had it, you
know. I put a box in my study specially for your dona-
tions. I knew you'd all rally round. Now, what about
it, Harry, old chap? You're the form captain. You

ought to give a lead. You might start it off with fifty pence.'

'I might, but on the other hand, I might not.'

'Stingy beast!' The Owl turned his attention to Bob Cherry. 'What about you, old man? You're not as mean as Wharton.'

'But I am. I'm worse,' grinned Bob, and there was more laughter.

'Or you, Johnny. I bet you've got fifty pence in your pocket.'

'That's right, and that's where it's going to stay.'

Bunter put his fat paw on Frank Nugent's arm. 'Frank, old fellow, you're generous—always have been. I've often said so. You wouldn't be stingy over fifty pence, would you?'

'Yes.'

'Beast! I say, Smithy—or what about you, Redwing?' Desperately, he grabbed at Toddy. 'Look, here, old chap. You ought to set the ball rolling. After all, we do share a study.'

Peter stared at him thoughtfully, and Bunter's hopes began to rise, and then his face became wreathed in smiles as Toddy said, 'Perhaps you're right. Maybe we should help. Look here, I'm going to drop something in the box, and I hope you'll follow suit.'

'Why should we help that fat bread basket? He should pay for what he pinched,' demanded Johnny.

'But I never!' hooted Bunter. 'And it wasn't worth ten quid anyway. I couldn't manage it all. Wasn't there. Anyway, one of the pears wasn't ripe.'

'Ha, ha, ha!' roared the juniors.

Bunter turned to Toddy. 'Go on, Toddy. Do what you said. Lead the way. I know you're a bit hard up so I don't mind if you can only spare a few pence. Poverty ain't a crime. It ain't your fault that your parents are poor.'

'Thanks,' said Peter. 'I appreciate that. That's why

I'm going to shove something in your box.' He turned round and gave the crowd a heavy wink, and there was a chuckle as they realised that whatever it was, it wasn't going to be what Bunter hoped for.

'You make me feel ashamed,' said Bob. 'I'll come with you, Toddy.'

'That's more like it,' beamed Bunter. 'Notes are best, but I won't turn anything down.'

'Sure?' asked Redwing, jingling some coins in his pocket.

'Certain, old man.'

Toddy marched up the passage with Bob Cherry close on his heels. Others followed them. Vernon-Smith took his wallet out of his pocket, and Bunter's little eyes gleamed. The Bounder was never short of cash.

'Play up!' he cried to the rest, shepherding them along the passage. 'Join in—that's the way. What about you, Skinner? After all, this is a special occasion.'

'He's right,' declared Skinner. 'Let's see what we can find, Snoop. Coming, Stott?'

'You don't want to be left out, do you, Fishy, old man?' asked Bunter.

Fisher T Fish chuckled. Although he never parted with money except on a business basis, he gave the Owl an affable nod. 'I guess I'm in on it. It sure is the bee's knees. Count me in, you fat clam.'

'Bolsover, Hazel, Field—off you go with Fishy,' said Bunter excitedly. 'What about you, Mauly? You're usually loaded. I hope you ain't going to be mean. Trot along with him Browney, and you, Ogilvy.'

By now there was no need for him to urge anyone to contribute to his fund. A wave of enthusiasm swept over them, and they poured up the passage to study no 7, forming quite a jam as fellows outside tried to force their way in, and those inside struggled to get out.

Bunter stood alone on the landing, blinking after

them. He had always thought that his appeal would have some effect, but he had no idea that it would be such a wild success. Everyone seemed to want to help. Visions of wealth floated before his dazzled eyes. There ought to be a fortune. He'd be able to pay Coker off and, with any luck, a happy and sticky fat Owl would be in the tuckshop the next day. He didn't know why there was so much laughter coming from his study, but he didn't care. The box was filling up, and that was all that mattered.

The mob of excited juniors came back towards the landing, laughing and shouting so loudly that they failed to hear rapid footsteps on the stairs.

'What is the meaning of this uproar?' There was a sudden silence as Mr Quelch reached the landing, and Bunter groaned and flashed a furious glance at his form master. It was just like Quelch to barge in at the wrong moment. 'What is going on, Wharton?'

'Oh—er, well, nothing, Mr Quelch.'

'Rubbish!' Quelch glanced round and then he spotted Bunter's notice on the wall. He strode across and peered at it. People shuffled their feet and looked anxiously at each other. Although they thought it was a joke, they didn't think Quelch would see it that way.

He swung round, astonished. 'Did you write this, Bunter?'

'Oh, sir!' mumbled the Owl. 'Er—yes, sir!'

'I have never seen anything like it! An appeal for money! This is disgraceful—absolutely disgraceful! Furthermore, it is the most badly written notice I have ever seen. Badly written, and badly spelled. I can hardly believe my eyes! You should be thoroughly ashamed of yourself.'

'But—but——'

'Have people made contributions, Bunter?'

'Oh, lor'! That is, yes, Mr Quelch,' said Bunter, miserably.

'Upon my word! You should have stopped this,

Wharton. You should have known that something like this cannot be permitted.'

'Oh, yes, Mr Quelch, but——'

'Did you put anything into the box yourself, Wharton?'

'Yes, but——'

Mr Quelch looked even more annoyed. 'You should not have done so, Wharton. As form captain, you should have set a better example. How many others have contributed?'

'Practically everyone, I think.'

'Appalling!' exclaimed Mr Quelch. 'This is quite absurd! I shall open the box and each of you will take back whatever you have contributed. Take down that ridiculous notice, Bunter.'

'But—but——'

'Immediately, Bunter!'

'Oh, lor'!' Miserably, he unpinned it, and shoved it into his blazer pocket.

'Follow me, Bunter. The rest of you will remain here.'

As Mr Quelch rustled into study no 7, Billy Bunter, his face downcast, trailed behind.

'Is that the box, Bunter?'

'Yes, sir.'

'I shall examine the contents, Bunter, and then——' Mr Quelch's voice died away as he lifted the lid of the biscuit tin. Billy Bunter saw his face twitch, and then he blinked at his form master once again. Quelch was actually laughing!

'Dear me! How absurd! Bunter, you ridiculous boy, you deserve this! You really do deserve it.'

'Eh? Do you mean—that is, mum—mum—may I keep it?'

Mr Quelch shook with laughter. 'Keep it? Of course you may,' he said, as he walked out of the study.

Bunter gaped after him, astonished. Whatever had made Quelch change his mind? Well, it didn't matter. The contents of the biscuit tin were his. He pounced—and a roar of baffled fury filled the air.

The box was almost full, but there were no notes and no coins. There were buttons, a chewed-up rubber, old envelopes, rubber bands, a marble, a broken penknife, pencil stubs, his own Latin dictionary, an empty ink bottle, toffee papers, and other odds and ends.

He gazed at that collection, an expression of total dismay on his fat face. Now he knew why Fishy had contributed. Now he knew why Skinner had trotted so willingly to his study, and why everyone had been so keen to join in.

'Beasts!' he yelled. 'Rotters!'

A roar of laughter came from the landing. Furiously, Bunter picked up the biscuit tin, and hurled it into the fireplace. There was a crash, and the contents spilled onto the floor. 'Beasts!' he roared.

Chapter 23
Raising the Cash

Fisher T Fish was busy in his study. It was a glorious afternoon. Fleecy clouds floated in a blue sky. Light breezes rustled the leaves of the elms. The faint sound of bat meeting ball could be heard through the open window, but blue skies and summer breezes and the pleasure of cricket were not strong enough to persuade Fishy to go out of doors.

He was sitting at his study table, counting his money and putting little piles of coins in orderly ranks. He was a business-like youth, keen and enterprising, with a very sharp eye for a bargain. There wasn't much scope in Greyfriars for anyone like Fishy, but he made the most of any opportunity that came his way.

He would buy and sell anything, and he always bought cheap and sold dear. He would lend small sums of money and charge interest. A chap who borrowed fifty pence would pay five pence a week interest until that fifty pence had been returned. Those who were hard up could sell their possessions to Fishy and then, when they were in the money again, they could buy them back for rather more than they had sold them. People might groan as they handed over their cash, but they couldn't do without him, and he knew it.

And so, as he counted his money, he wasn't pleased when the study door opened and a pair of large, round specs glimmered in. He waved a bony hand in dismissal. 'Beat it!' he said, tersely.

'Oh, really, Fishy——'

'Out, at the double! Shut the door!'

William George was not the kind of customer that Fisher T Fish welcomed. The Owl would happily have raised a loan at any rate of interest on the understanding that it would be repaid out of his next postal order, but Fishy had never been keen on the deal. Bunter really couldn't think why.

'Beat it!' said Fishy again.

However, Bunter didn't beat it. As he rolled into the study, Fishy looked for something to hurl at him, but then he saw that he had a cricket bat under one arm and a stack of books under the other. Immediately, Fishy dropped the cushion.

'Say, what have you got?' Fishy wasn't going to lend the Owl a cent, but he was open for business.

Bunter blinked at him. 'I'm in a fix, Fishy. It's that ten quid. That sordid beast Quelch has just mentioned it again. The only way I can raise the wind is to sell a few things. Take a look at this bat, Fishy.

FISHY WASN'T GOING TO LEND THE OWL A CENT, BUT HE
WAS OPEN FOR BUSINESS.

It's a good one. Even you can see that. My father paid about fifteen pounds for it.'

'He was robbed!'

'I'll—I'll let you have it for five. How about that?'

'Nope!'

'Four?' said Bunter, hopefully.

'Nope!'

'Then how much? It's a jolly good one. Come on, Fishy. What'll you pay? You've got me over a barrel. I must have the money.'

'I know,' grinned Fishy. 'I'll give you a couple of quid.'

'What?' hooted Bunter. 'I don't know what Toddy would say!'

'What's it got to do with Toddy?'

'Oh, oh! nothing. It's—it's just that he's always admired it,' said Bunter, hastily. 'Can't you make it two fifty, Fishy?'

'Nope,'

'You're a hard man.'

'Yep. Take it or leave it.'

The Owl sighed. 'Okay.' He handed over the bat, and Fishy put it on the floor. 'Now what about these books?' Bunter dumped them on the carpet.

Fishy examined the pile, and shook his head. 'These are a drag on the market right now,' he said, disparagingly. 'They're in a lousy condition.'

'But Fishy,' said Bunter, persuasively. 'Chaps are always losing books. You know that you can sell them.'

'I'm loaded with books.'

'But—but look at this Latin dictionary——'

'All right. Ten pence a book.'

'Ten pence? Is that all?'

'Yep,' said Fishy, firmly.

'Beast! All right, it's a deal.' Bunter knew when he was defeated. As Fishy dumped the books on the floor, Bunter pulled out a set of geometry instruments.

'What about these?'

'Where's the box for them?' demanded Fishy.

'Didn't—didn't bring it. Didn't think you'd want it. It's—it's got my name on. But they're worth quite a lot. Look at the compasses. Sharp as anything.'

'Fifty pence the lot,' said Fishy, briskly.

'All right.' Bunter breathed hard. Raising the wind was hard going. 'What have I got so far? Two fifty for the bat——'

'Two, not two fifty.'

'Oh, yes. And twelve books at ten pence each makes another one fifty, and fifty for these makes four fifty. Call it five quid, and I'll see what else I can rake up.'

'Three seventy,' said Fishy. 'That's what it comes to, and that's what you'll get.'

'Oh!' The Owl fumbled in a pocket, and brought out a small clock. 'This is the best on the market,' he said, earnestly. 'It's a travelling alarm.'

'So what?'

'So it's worth heaps of money. It's got a leather case, Fishy.'

'A quid.'

'Mean beast.' From his top pocket, Bunter produced a fountain pen. 'This is silver,' he said impressively.

Fishy examined it. 'That's not silver, you dope. Anyway, who uses fountain pens these days?'

'Wharton does,' said Bunter, promptly.

Fishy looked at him sharply. 'What's that got to do with it?'

'I—I only meant that Wharton's uncle gave him one just like it. Cost about five pounds, I believe.'

'You're joking! Fifty pence.'

'But you'll be able to flog it for more than that,' said the Owl, indignantly.

Fishy gave a thin smile. 'Sure. That's why I'm buying it.'

'Stingy beast. How much have I got now?'

'Five pounds twenty.'

Bunter next offered Fishy a large pocket knife. 'This is smashing!' he said. 'It's got five blades and a corkscrew and a screwdriver and——'

'Thirty pence,' said Fishy, briefly.

'What? But Bob Cherry said——'

'Who cares what Bob Cherry said?'

The negotiations continued. A small transistor radio brought quite a lot of money, and a pocket calculator did quite well too, but an old wallet and some sunglasses did rather badly. The pile of goods at Fishy's feet became quite large.

'Anything else?' demanded Fishy.

'Have we got up to ten pounds?' asked Bunter, anxiously.

'Yep.'

'Can you give it to me straight away?' asked the Owl. 'I'm—I'm in a bit of a hurry. Got to see Quelch.' As Fishy slowly counted out the money, he began to look worried as he heard the sound of activity in the passage outside. 'Get a move on,' he said.

Chapter 24

Stolen Goods

'Hang on,' said Peter Todd. 'I'll nip into my study and get my bat.'

'Okay,' said Bob.

'Make it snappy,' urged Harry Wharton.

Toddy disappeared, and Vernon-Smith came out of his study. 'Coming down to the nets?' asked Bob.

Smithy shook his head. 'Can't.' He held up an empty box. 'Some fool's been in my study. My geometry instruments are gone. You didn't borrow them, did you?'

'Not guilty,' said Bob.

'Well, I've got to find them,' frowned Smithy. 'Lascelles wants that extra work from me. If Bunter's borrowed them again, I'll scalp him.'

'Get a move on, Toddy!' shouted Harry.

'But I can't find my bat.' As Bob and Harry made their way to study no 7, they could hear him saying, 'Seen my bat, Tom?'

'Your hat? I expect it's in the cloakroom.'

'Not my hat, Tom. My bat.'

'What cat?'

Bob appeared in the doorway and saw Tom standing by the bookcase. 'He's looking for his cricket bat, Tom.'

Tom Dutton didn't hear. 'Where's my Latin dictionary?'

There was a shout from the corridor. 'Did you borrow my radio, Wharton?' Johnny Bull stomped down the passage.

'No. Why?'

'You said you'd like to know what the test score is.'

'But I'd have asked you first.'

'Well, some clown's got it.'

'Somebody's borrowed my geometry instruments,' said the Bounder, grimly. 'If I get my hands on him——'

'There's been quite a lot of borrowing going on,' remarked Bob. 'Toddy's bat, Tom's dictionary——'

'Who's got my bat?' shouted Toddy.

'What for?' asked Tom.

'So I can play cricket, you fool.'

A look of understanding appeared on Tom's face. 'Oh, you want your cricket bat?'

'Of course I do.'

'Then ask Bunter.'

'Why?'

'I saw him with one. He'd got a pile of books as well. I wonder if he picked up my dictionary.'

'Where did he go?' demanded Toddy.

'He went into Fishy's study. If you see him, ask him about my Latin dictionary.'

The small crowd sped off to study no 14, and Toddy threw the door open with a crash. Fisher T Fish, who was still counting out money, looked up in surprise. 'Snake's eggs! What the——?'

'Oh, pancakes! Oh, peppermints!' squawked Bunter. 'I—I say, Toddy, push off. Me and Fishy was having a little chat. You're interrupting.'

'Where's my bat?' demanded Toddy.

'Eh? Your bat? I—I don't know. Why should I? Ask—ask Wharton. I—I've got a feeling that he borrowed it.'

Harry appeared in the doorway. 'Think again, fat man.'

'Oh! I—I didn't know you were there, Harry, old chap. No, no. It wasn't Harry. As I was saying, Johnny Bull just tucked it under his arm and——'

Johnny elbowed his way to the front of the group. 'Oh, yes?' he said, a threatening look on his face.

'Yes—that is, what I meant was no. Or—or——' The fat Owl looked alarmed as more fellows joined the crowd. 'It—it wasn't you, Johnny. Not you at all. It—it was someone in the fourth. Temple. I remember. Temple borrowed it.'

Johnny pointed to the floor. 'Isn't that your bat, Toddy?'

Toddy marched in, his face red with anger. He grabbed it, and turned to the Owl. 'You fat filcher! You crooked cuttlefish! What's it doing here?'

'Who? Me? I—er—I——'

'Take your hands off that!' snapped Fishy. 'That's mine.'

'No, it isn't! it's mine.'

'Think again, wise guy. I've paid good cash for that.'

'What?' shrieked Toddy.

'I gave him a couple of quid for it.'

'You—you——' Toddy became speechless.

'The fat man's just sold me a load of things.'

Bob bent down. 'I say, Fishy, what are doing with my pocket knife?'

'Yours? It's mine.'

Bob took no notice. 'Johnny, this is remarkably like your transistor.' He piled all the goods onto the table.

Smithy snatched up the geometry instruments. 'These are mine.'

Fishy tried to grab them back. 'No. They're mine now. I gave fifty pence.'

'Fifty pence!' snarled the Bounder. 'You're nearly as big a villain as he is.'

'Here is my calculator,' said Hurree Singh, 'and this fountain pen is like yours, Harry.'

'Mine!' shouted Harry. 'You—you rotten bloodsucker, Bunter.'

'No!' squeaked Bunter. 'I—I—that is, it wasn't me—just a joke—knew Fishy would give them back. He said, that is——' He became incoherent. 'Never did, found them——'

Fishy looked at the cash that he had counted out. 'I guess you guys came in the nick of time. I was just going to give that walking hamburger ten quid.'

'You pirate, Bunter!'

'Scrag him!'

'Scalp him!'

'Burst him!'

'I—I say——' Bunter dodged round the table in alarm. 'Lemme explain. You don't think I'd—keep that bat away, Toddy, you beast! If you kick me again, Smithy, I'll—yaroooop! I say—listen! Lemme explain——'

'I'm going to give you a taste of this bat!' roared Toddy.

'Yarooo! Keep off, you beast!' shrieked Bunter.

'Stop jabbing me with those compasses, Smithy, you rotter! Ouch! I—I only borrowed your things, just for a day or two. Shouldn't have let me down over my fund. Only borrowed them to tide me over. Tain't dishonest—intended to buy them back, you beasts!'

'Oh, and where's the money coming from?' asked the Bounder.

'Postal order—from one—one of my titled relations,' babbled Bunter.

'What!'

'Collar him!' roared Bob.

'Bag him!'

'Bump him!'

'Oh, crikey! Leggo! I say, you fellows—beasts! Stoppit, Smithy! If you kick me again, Wharton—leggo my ear, Bull! Stop poking me with that bat, Toddy—Ow! Ow! Wow! Help! Yaroop!'

Billy Bunter had come to raise the wind, but what he'd raised was a whirlwind. Squealing and squawking, he escaped into the passage and fled wildly up the passage.

'Whew!' Fisher T Fish wiped his forehead. 'That was a near thing. That shark nearly got ten quid out of me.'

'There's another shark here!' said Toddy, grimly. 'Who said my bat's only worth a couple of quid?' He looked round. 'Who's going to lend a hand?'

'What do you mean?' asked Fishy, nervously.

'I'll show you!'

'What? Oh, Christopher Columbus. Don't——'

He was too late. Hands shot out. Fishy was lifted high in the air, the hands were removed, and he crashed onto the floor of his study. The table rocked, and the piles of coins showered over him. 'Ouch!' he groaned, and wondered why they had picked on an honest trader.

Chapter 25
Sporting!

'Is there a letter for me?'

'Yes!'

'Oh, good!' exclaimed Billy Bunter.

Bunter trundled along to the letter rack every day, hoping that his long-awaited postal order might have arrived at last. He wasn't interested in any letter that might accompany it. He didn't want to know how his parents were, and he didn't want to know what they had been doing. All he wanted was cash, and he had never wanted it as much as he did now. Quelch was demanding that ten quid. Now, seeing a letter, he felt a flicker of hope.

'Pass it over, Cherry.'

'Don't tell me that you've got your postal order,' grinned Smithy, 'the one you've been expecting ever since you got here.'

'Oh, really, Smithy——'

'From one of your titled relations?' asked Skinner. 'Which one? The duke or the marquis?'

'Yah!' Bunter glanced at the envelope, and his expression changed from one of happy expectation to one of gloom. He recognised the writing. It was from his father, and his father never sent cash. He wrote about money, but only to urge his son to economise. No postal orders or pound notes ever tumbled from his envelope.

The Owl saw that Smithy had a letter, and he felt even gloomier. Smithy often received money. It just didn't seem fair. An idea shot into his head. 'I—I say, Smithy!'

Smithy glanced at his envelope, turned it over, and shoved it into his blazer pocket. 'Yes?'

'Look here, Smithy. We've each got a letter, and

neither of us have opened them. You're a sportsman, aren't you? Well, I'll make you a sporting offer.'

The Bounder stared at him. 'What are you getting at?'

'Listen!' said Billy Bunter, impatiently. 'As I said, we've both got a letter. There might be cash in yours. Right? Well, there might be cash in mine. What I'm saying is, let's share. Go half each.'

'You must be joking!'

'No, I'm not. It's a sporting offer like I said. Ten to one there's money in one of the letters. If it's in yours, then you share with me. If it's in mine, then I'll share with you. What could be fairer that that?'

'How sporting!' said Hurree Singh. 'It's heads Bunter wins and tails Smithy loses.' There was a burst of laughter.

'Stop cackling!' said Bunter crossly. 'It's a fair offer. After all, I'm as likely to have money as Smithy——'

'Of course,' said Bob, keeping a straight face. 'What about it, Smithy. You know how likely it is that Bunter's got his postal order. You could be onto a good thing.'

'Ha, ha, ha!'

'Shut up, you fools!' hooted Bunter. 'Smithy, old man, now's the chance to prove you're a sportsman.'

Smithy nodded. 'Okay, fat man,' he said. 'I'll do it. Let's get it straight. We'll open our envelopes, and if there's any cash, we split it.

'Right!' Bunter could hardly believe his luck.

Smithy looked round. 'You're all witnesses,' he said.

'You must be heading for the bin, Smithy,' said Peter Todd. 'He's as likely to have a postal order as he is to sprout wings.'

'Shut up, Toddy!' howled Bunter, fearful that Smithy might change his mind. 'Stop interfering. Smithy's given his word, and he won't back out.' He blinked anxiously through his specs. 'You won't, will you, old man?'

'I've no intention of backing out,' said the Bounder, coolly.

'You open first,' said Billy Bunter. 'Hurry up, Smithy.'

'All right.' Vernon-Smith drew his envelope from his pocket, and slit it open with his penknife. He drew out a folded piece of paper and handed it to Bunter. 'Here you are. You can open it.'

'Thanks.' Bunter's hands were shaking with excitement. 'Oh!' he gasped as he read the message. The eager expression faded, and the paper fluttered to the ground.

Bob picked it up, glanced at it, and then he laughed. 'Hard luck, fat man. Smithy's got a bill.'

'That's right. I had my bike repaired.'

'Oh, crikey!' burst out Bunter. 'You—you beast, Smithy. Tain't from your family at all.'

'Is that what you thought?' drawled the Bounder, a faint smile on his lips.

'Of course I did. You didn't say it wasn't. Anyway, how did you know it was a bill? You didn't even look at it.'

'I didn't have to.' Smithy showed Bunter the back of the envelope. 'It's got Brown's Cycles stamped on it.'

'But—but—it ain't fair. You—you jolly well knew——'

'Come on, Bunter,' urged Skinner. 'Open up.'

Billy Bunter gave an angry grunt, jabbed his thumb into the envelope, and ripped it open. He drew out a letter and unfolded it. 'Oh, crumbs!' He gave a startled gasp.

Bob looked over his shoulder. 'I can't believe it! It's a postal order!

'Never!' exclaimed Harry.

'Oh, crikey! Oh, acid drops!'

'Hold me up, Frank!' cried Bob. 'It's for ten quid.'

'Well, well, well,' murmured the Bounder. 'What a

stroke of luck. That'll be five pounds each.'

Billy Bunter stood there, staring at the postal order. He had never had so much money in his life before, and now he had to share it with Smithy. It was a bitter thought. The Bounder gave a quiet chuckle. He had only been pulling the Owl's leg when he had agreed to the sporting offer. Now he could pull it for a little longer.

'Ten quid!' muttered Bunter. 'Ten quid!'

'It's lucky you're dealing with a sportsman,' said Bob.

'You bet,' agreed Smithy. 'Half each, Bunter.'

'Eh, What?'

'Halves, Bunter.'

'But—but—but I say, Smithy, it—it was only a joke——'

That's where you're wrong.'

'But, Smithy, old man——'

'I wasn't joking. I meant it.'

'Serves you right,' said Toddy. 'You hoped to make something out of Smithy. Well, the boot's on the other foot. You've diddled yourself.'

'You'll have to pay up,' declared Bob.

'We'll go and cash it later on,' said Smithy.

Bunter's fat paws clutched the postal order. 'I—I—I say——'

'There's no need to say anything, old porpoise.'

'But—but—I never knew. Didn't think——'

'That's your bad luck,' said Smithy.

The Owl glanced round the circle of grinning faces. 'Oh—oh, just a tick, Smithy. Haven't read my letter.'

There was laughter at Bunter's tactics. He was clearly playing for time, hoping that the bell would ring for lessons.

'Who sent the money?' asked Bob.

'It's an—an advance birthday present,' mumbled Bunter. 'It's from my Uncle George.' He became indignant. 'My father says it's too much. He says I ought to save it. Huh!' Normally, if he had bothered to read the letter at all, he would have crumpled it up and thrown it away, but now he re-read it, and sighed with relief as the bell rang.

'Come on,' said Harry. 'Quelch will get ruffled if we're late.'

'That's right,' agreed Bunter eagerly. 'Don't want to miss history,' and there was another roar of laughter as he shot away.

Chapter 26
Just Like Quelch

If Quelch had been waiting outside the form room, Bunter would have been delighted for once, but he was disappointed, and he blinked uneasily as Smithy and the rest of the Remove arrived.

Bunter wasn't good at thinking, otherwise he would have realised that Smithy didn't want his money, but as it was, he thrust his postal order deeper into his pocket, determined that it should stay there until he reached the tuckshop. Mrs Mimble was always willing to change postal orders if some of the cash was to be spent in her shop.

'You'll have to cough up,' said Skinner.

'I—I know, but I—I say, Smithy, can I let you have it out of my next postal order? It's—it's coming any day now.'

'No!'

'But—but it'll probably be in the post tomorrow.'

'Don't think I doubt your word, but a bird in the hand——'

'Oh! Well—well, I'll see you after class.'

'And I'll see you,' said the Bounder, meaningly.

'I—I say, Smithy, I'm not trying to get out of it, but I—I've got to pay Coker. It's a debt of honour. We Bunters never forget debts of honour.'

'Good. This is one,' said Smithy, poker faced.

'I—I can't go on owing Coker money, Smithy. It's—it's not the sort of thing that I can do. I tell you what. I'll hand over my next postal order—all of it.'

'Sh!' hissed Bob. 'Our Henry's coming.'

'Can't do anything about it now,' whispered Bunter to Smithy, and went thankfully into the form room.

As the lesson went on, the Owl's brow became more and more thoughtful. The cash had come and he was eager to see it go, but not to Smithy or Quelch. He wanted it to disappear into Mrs Mimble's till. There was so much that could be done with that amount of money, and he could think of nothing else. He wriggled with impatience while Quelch continued the history lesson.

'Name a battle won by the Royalists during the civil war, Wharton.'

'Brentford, Mr Quelch.'

'Quite right. And who led the Royalists, Bunter?'

There was silence. The fat Owl wasn't aware that he had been spoken to. His mind was on doughnuts.

'Bunter!' Mr Quelch raised his voice. 'Who led them?'

For a moment, Bunter hardly knew where he was or what he had been asked. 'A—a postal order, sir!'

The howl of laughter died as Quelch frowned around the room. 'What was that?' he demanded, raising his eyebrows.

'Oh, oh! No, not that. Didn't mean, that is——'

'Be quiet, Bunter. Obviously, you haven't the slightest idea of what we have been talking about. You were thinking about something else. What was it?'

'It—it—it wasn't doughnuts, not——'

'Doughnuts?' Quelch's eyebrows were raised even higher.

'Yes. No. That is, not exactly.'

'What do you mean?'

'I—I'm not really keen on—on doughnuts. That is, I—I am, specially if they're fresh. I—I didn't know Mrs Mimble had got a new lot in. I wasn't wondering if she'd got any left, and——'

'That is quite enough!' rasped Mr Quelch. 'And now perhaps you will tell me what you know about Brentford.'

'Brentford?' Bunter was puzzled. Quelch had got it wrong again. Here he was, talking about geography again instead of history. 'I—er—I——'

'Well?'

'It—it's near London.'

'Yes. What else do you know about it?'

Bunter racked his brain. 'It—it's got a—a school and a—a football team, and—and you go past it when you're going north to places like Cornwall and Wales.'

The class rocked with laughter while Quelch gazed at Bunter in disbelief. Bunter glared indignantly round the room. 'You lot can jolly well shut up. I went there once. I jolly well know where it is. One of my titled relations lives near there in Southend.'

Mr Quelch leaned across his desk. 'Bunter. There was a battle at Brentford. What can you tell me about it?'

'Oh!' said Bunter blankly. He cast about in his fat mind for something to say.

'I am waiting, Bunter.'

'It—it was a bit of a scrap, sir, that's what it was. Was—was it after a soccer match——?' His voice died away as he saw Quelch's angry frown. 'No, no, I—I didn't mean that,' he said quickly. 'I—I was thinking——'

'Then what did you mean?'

'It—it was a battle between—between——'

121

'Bunter! I am trying to control my temper. Tell me, who commanded the Royalists at the battle of Brentford?'

'I—er—w—was it Mont—Montgomery, sir?'

'Montgomery!' thundered Mr Quelch.

'Nun-no, not Montgomery,' said the fat Owl hastily. 'It—it was Nelson, that's who it was, and he sent that message. You know the one, sir. England expects every man to have a postal order.'

Mr Quelch took a deep breath. 'You will stay in after class this afternoon, Bunter, and you will remain here until you have written out fifty times that Prince Rupert of the Rhine commanded the Royalist troops at the battle of Brentford.'

'Oh, lor'! Oh, crikey!'

'And if your attention wanders again, I shall cane you.'

'Oh, crumbs!' He sat listening intently for the rest of the lesson, but as soon as the bell rang, he leaped from his seat and made for the door.

'Bunter!' rapped Mr Quelch.

'Oh!'

'Do not forget those lines, Bunter, and bring them to me this evening. And there is the matter of the money you owe Coker. Have you received it yet? If not, I shall write to your father. Did the letter you received this morning contain money?'

'Did—did I get one, sir? I—I can't quite——'

'You did. I put the letters in the rack myself, and I saw from the postmark that yours came from home.'

'I—well, that is——'

'If you have ten pounds, give it to me.'

Bunter gave a dismal blink through the big, round specs, and reluctantly handed over his precious postal order.

Mr Quelch glanced at it. 'This is made out in your name, Bunter. As soon as classes are over this morning, go and cash it at the post office.

Eagerly, the fat Owl took it back and stuffed it into a sticky pocket, and he chuckled as Mr Quelch left the form room.

Chapter 27
Pay Up Bunter

'Bob, old chap!'

'What do you want?' Bob Cherry came to a halt as Bunter's fat hand grasped his arm.

'I—I say,' said the Owl nervously. 'Smithy's waiting in the quad.'

'So what?' Bob glanced out, and saw Vernon-Smith standing near the door, talking to Redwing and Hazeldene. 'What about it, fatty?'

'I—I think he's waiting for me. He wants to get his hands on his share of my postal order.'

Bob laughed. 'Don't be such a fat fool. Smithy was only pulling your leg. He wouldn't pick up your postal order with a pair of tongs.'

'It—it's not that I won't settle with Smithy. I will. It's a debt of honour. A deal is a deal. I wouldn't dream of backing out—but I'll have to do it later. You know, when the post has come.'

'Dry up, clothhead!'

'Beast—no, no. Listen to me, Bob, old man. I—I say, I bet you could beat Smithy in a scrap, couldn't you?'

'What for?'

'You could lick him easily,' said Bunter, flatteringly. 'You're the best boxer in the form. And you're plucky. We all know that. You wouldn't mind taking on a worm like Smithy, would you? I—I say, if you lick him, I'll—I'll stand you some sausage rolls, honestly I will.'

'What have you got in place of a brain, Bunter? Cotton wool?'

'Oh, really, Cherry! Don't think I want you to lick Smithy while I nip into the tuckshop without being spotted, do you? No, nothing like that. I was riled at what he said about you. Insulting, that's what it was. Downright insulting.'

'Like what?' asked Bob.

'Like—like you're a lumbering lunatic with the biggest feet in Greyfriars. He said that there wasn't room for anyone else once your feet were inside the study.'

'Really?'

'Really, and he said worse than that. He said that you can't play cricket for toffee, that you handle a bat like a shovel, and you stand about like a sack of coal when you're fielding. Talk about insults! I know what I'd do to anyone who said that about me. I'd——'

'And I know what I'll do,' said Bob, grimly. 'I'm going to kick him from one side of the quad to the other.'

'Quite right,' agreed Bunter, eagerly. 'You jolly well ought to kick him and lick him all over the place. By the way, I forgot to say that he said you'd got a voice like a megaphone and face like a Turkey carpet.'

'Nice of you to tell me. Believe me, I'll deal with the bloke who said that.'

'Good for you,' said Bunter.

'Right!' Bob's arm shot out. He grabbed the Owl by his collar and swung him round.

'Ow! Leggo! Wharrer you up to? Gone off your head, Cherry? Stoppit, you great ape!'

'I'm doing what you said. I'm kicking the bloke who said all those things about me.'

'Yarooop! Ow! Beast! Whoops!'

Bob chuckled, and went on his way, but the fat

Owl remained just inside the doorway, wriggling uncomfortably, his eyes fixed on the Bounder. In spite of everything that Bob had said, he was still convinced that Smithy was waiting to pounce on him.

He started as someone tapped him on the shoulder. 'Out of the way, jumbo,' said Harry Wharton cheerfully. 'You're blocking the doorway.'

'I—I say!' squeaked Billy Bunter. 'Have a word with Smithy. Quelch wants to see him in his study.'

'Oh? When did you see Quelch?'

'Just a short time ago. He popped out, and said he wanted Smithy straight away.'

Harry laughed. 'I must be getting deaf. I've only just left Quelch. I didn't hear him mention Smithy.'

'Did I say Quelch?' said Bunter, quickly. 'Silly of me. I—I meant Lascelles. He—he wants to see Smithy about his maths.'

'Clever old Lascelles,' remarked Harry. 'I wonder how he manages it?'

'Manages what?'

'To be in two places at once. I happen to know he's doing a spot of coaching on the playing field.'

'Oh!' The Owl tried again. 'I'm getting forgetful, Harry, old man. It was Dr Locke who wanted him. You ought to tell him straight away. Mustn't keep the head waiting. I—I say, don't walk away while I'm talking!' and he scowled as Harry drifted off.

He hovered in the doorway, and then jumped like a startled rabbit as the Bounder walked in. 'Oh, I—I say, Smithy!' he gasped. 'Quelch—I mean Lascalles, that is, the head—they all want you on the cricket ground. I—I mean——'

'You clot!' said Smithy. 'Why haven't you gone to the post office?'

'Eh?'

'If you get a move on, you can get to Friardale and back before lunch. The sooner you hand the cash to Quelch, the better.'

'Oh! I—I thought——' It began to dawn on the Owl that Smithy didn't want his share of the money. 'Don't—don't you want a fiver?'

'Of course I don't, you fat bandit. Now, get moving!'

'Righto. Straight away,' said Bunter, and he rolled off, grinning from ear to ear. He rolled across the quad, and rolled towards the tuckshop.

'Oh, here you are!'

Bunter blinked at Peter Todd, standing in the doorway. 'Yes,' he said, doubtfully. 'Like—like a sausage roll, Peter? I'm going to stand you one.'

'No, you're not,' said Peter. 'You're coming for a walk with me, old cheesecake.' He linked a lean arm in Bunter's fat one. 'This way!'

'No! I don't want to go for a walk. Leggo, you beast! Wharrer you up to?'

'We're going for a nice little stroll to Friardale.'

'No, I'm not!' Bunter gave Toddy a glare of concentrated fury.

'Your mistake,' said Peter. 'You are!'

'You mind your own business, Peter Todd!'

'This is my business. The chaps have made me your keeper. Come on. I'm taking your arm for a walk.' Peter marched off with Bunter's arm, and the Owl accompanied it. A parting would have been painful.

Bunter was crimson with fury as they made their way out of the school and down the lane to Friardale, and he told Toddy over and over again what he thought of him, but Peter remained unmoved by threats, pleas and offers of bribery.

When they reached the post office, Peter stopped. 'Where's the postal order?' he asked.

Bunter clapped a podgy hand to his mouth. 'Oh, golly!' he exclaimed. 'Silly of me, Toddy. I—I left it in the study.'

'Sure it isn't in your pocket?'

'No.'

... AND PETER MARCHED HIM INSIDE.

'Perhaps you should make certain,' said Toddy, 'because I shall bang your fat head against this wall until you find it.'

'Beast!' Realising that he had no alternative, Bunter produced the crumpled postal order, and Peter marched him inside.

A few minutes later, they emerged again, and Toddy grasped the fat Owl's arm once more and wheeled him off in the direction of school.

'I—I say, Toddy,' said Bunter, as they neared Greyfriars, 'there's no need to come to Quelch with me. I know you want to get in some cricket.' They turned in at the gates, and made their way across the quad.

'I'll have plenty of time,' said Toddy.

'But—but I don't want to be a nuisance.'

'But you're not.' Toddy piloted him along the masters' corridor. 'Lift your plates of meat,' he said, as the Owl's footsteps slowed down, and he tugged Bunter's arm.

'Ouch! That hurt! Leggo!'

'Won't be long.' Toddy dragged the reluctant Owl to the door of Quelch's study, and tapped on the door.

'Come in,' said Mr Quelch, and Toddy shoved Bunter inside.

'Beast!' hissed Bunter, turning around and shooting a look of blistering hatred at him.

Quelch looked up. 'Oh, it's you, Bunter. 'You've been rather a long time. Put the money on my desk, please.'

Sadly, the Owl put the little wad of notes onto the desk, gave it a last, dismal blink and left the study. 'Beast! Rotter! Tick!' he said bitterly to Toddy, who was still hovering in the corridor.

The fact that he had been saved from yet another row didn't enter Bunter's head. He was mourning the loss of the food that had been almost within his grasp. It wasn't until the bell rang for lunch that the cloud of gloom lifted and, as he rolled into the dining room and smelt steak and kidney pudding, he brightened up at last. Life, he decided, was worth living after all.

Chapter 28
A Friend in Need

'Why not Bunter?' murmured Harry Wharton.

'Eh?'

'What?'

Four members of the Famous Five looked in astonishment at the fifth. Over tea they had been discussing the forthcoming cricket match against Highcliffe.

'Did you say Bunter?' asked Johnny Bull.

'Yep.'

'Are you joking?' said Bob. 'We were talking about cricket. Like oil and water, they don't mix.'

'We need a good side against Highcliffe,' remarked Johnny.

Harry laughed. 'I wasn't thinking of Highcliffe. I was thinking of the game against the fourth tomorrow. They're so rotten we could beat them without even trying. Well, since Bunter's so keen to be included——'

Johnny snorted. 'Keen? Not that porker!'

'I know he's a lazy toad,' admitted Harry, 'but he'd jump at the chance, especially since Quelch might come and watch.'

'It would be like playing ten men,' remarked Frank.

'But we could still beat them.'

'I don't see it,' argued Johnny. 'He's a slug and a wart. Why should he be in the team?'

'But he really is up against it,' said Harry. 'Quelch is fed up with him——'

'And so am I.'

'It wouldn't hurt us to give him a hand.'

'I wouldn't mind so much if he did something to help himself,' remarked Frank.

Harry grinned. 'He does. He helps himself only too often.'

'You're telling me,' said Bob. 'He tried to help himself to one of my apples yesterday.'

'We can't help him in class,' Frank said. 'I tried to persuade him that Canada isn't the capital of the United States, but he wouldn't believe me.'

'It might help if we put him in the team. It might cheer Quelch up.'

'I rather think that it will cheer up the fourth,' put in Hurree Singh.

'You never know,' Harry went on. 'He might even get a run or two.'

'And pigs might fly,' growled Johnny.

'He might even take a catch.'

'He's even more likely to drop one,' Frank pointed out.

Johnny frowned. 'It doesn't seem right to me. Other chaps——'

'Oh, come on, Johnny,' said Harry. 'Let's give that bladder of lard a chance. It won't hurt us. We're going to win anyway.'

'Cricket's cricket,' said Johnny, stubbornly. 'Why should we throw away a wicket?'

'Why shouldn't we?' asked Bob. 'It'll give him a bit of a lift.

'Well——'

'Oh, all right,' said Johnny, grudgingly.

'I'm going to be in the Rag when Harry puts up the team,' said Frank. 'I can't wait to hear what people will say.' He looked up as the door opened. 'Here's the man of the moment.'

Billy Bunter blinked at them. 'Hallo, you chaps.'

'Roll in, old barrel,' said Bob.

'You're the bread basket I was hoping to see,' remarked Harry.

Bunter bowled in, his eyes scanning the table. 'What, no tea?' he said in a disappointed voice. 'Have you greedy beasts finished it all? Got anything in the cupboard?'

'No!' snapped Johnny.

'Just stop thinking about your stomach,' said Harry. 'I want to talk to you about cricket.'

'Oh, is that all? I thought you meant——'

'Well, I didn't. I've decided to play you in the eleven. You'll be able to show Quelch that you're not quite such a clot as he thinks.'

'Oh!' sniffed Bunter. 'It's taken you long enough, Wharton. I'm not sure that I can play,' he said, loftily. 'You've left me out of the team all through the term, and now you suddenly need me. Well, I'm not sure that I can make it.'

Harry looked so astonished that the rest of the Famous Five burst out laughing.

'Oh, you can cackle,' said Bunter, warmly, 'but that's the way I see it. I've been passed over, left out and ignored—me the best cricketer in the form, and now you can't do without me. Well, I'll have to think about it. Mind you, I'm not saying that I won't play.'

There was another burst of laughter. 'I do wish you'd stop sounding like a lot of hyenas,' said Bunter, peevishly.

'Well, you don't have to play,' said Harry.

'I—I think I'd better,' said Billy Bunter, quickly. 'I—I can't let the form down, and you do need me. Highcliffe aren't a bad side, are they, and they give you a jolly good tea afterwards. Yes, you put my name down. Wharton.'

'Ha, ha, ha!'

You great gargoyle!' shouted Harry. 'You don't

think I'm going to play you against Highcliffe, do you?'

'Oh! Which one then? I'd rather play at home, but I happen to know that Quelch is going to walk over to Highcliffe. The sooner he sees me in action, the better.'

'You silly chump!' roared Harry. 'The only team you're playing in is the one against the fourth tomorrow.'

Bunter blinked indignantly at him. 'Look here, Wharton. I'm not wasting my talent on game like that. It's Highcliffe or nothing.

'Okay, then it's nothing. Now roll out before I kick you out!'

'Oh, really Wharton!'

'Shove off!'

'Oh! Oh, I—I say—' stammered the Owl, now anxious not to let the opportunity slip away. 'I—I guess I'll play. It's—it's better than nothing.'

'Clear off! Shut the door behind you.'

'But—but I don't think you understand, Harry, old chap. I'm—I'm fearfully keen to play. Quelch will like seeing me knock up a century.'

'It might take a number of centuries before you achieve that, my dear Bunter.'

'Yah! You're just jealous because I'm a better cricketer than you.' The Owl turned to Harry again. 'I'll play. You can count on me. Mind you, I'll have to cancel my previous engagements. It's quite a strain, being so popular. But still, don't worry. I'll be there.'

As the Owl rolled away, Harry glared while the others just grinned.

'It's no good being mad, Harry,' said Bob. 'It was your idea. You'd better start making out the list.'

'I've got a good mind to leave him out.'

'You can't,' said Frank. 'You said you wanted to give him a hand.'

'I suppose I'll put him in,' muttered Harry.

Half an hour later, he posted the team in the Rag. A small crowd collected, and at first there was a stunned silence as they saw W G Bunter at the bottom of the list, and then there was a shout of laughter.

The Owl strutted into the common room, and stood importantly by the notice board. 'Why are you cackling?' he asked. 'Is it because Cherry's in again?'

There was another burst of laughter. 'You bloated bullfrog!' shouted Bob.

'I know what it is, Cherry,' sneered Bunter. 'You don't want to be shown up by me. Once I get my hands on a bat——'

'You'll brain anyone within striking distance,' said Skinner.

Vernon-Smith entered the Rag, and looked at the team list. 'Is it a joke, Wharton?' he asked. 'Is Bunter really playing?'

'Yes. Don't worry. We can beat them even if we were a man short.'

'And that's what it comes to.'

'You'd like to keep me in the shade, wouldn't you?' jeered Bunter. 'You're afraid that I'll do well and you'll be dropped.

The Bounder grinned. 'I'm terrified.'

'I've put Bunter in for his batting,' said Harry, cheerfully. 'Lesser lights like Hurree and Browney can take care of the bowling.'

'That won't do, Wharton!' said the Owl, firmly.

'What?'

'I said it won't do. I know I'm a good bat, but I can bowl, you know. I wouldn't claim to be first-class——'

'No?' said Bob, in mock surprise.

'Hurree's almost as good as I am.'

'Thanks awfully.'

'And Browney's all right, I suppose——'

'That's good of you, fat man.'

'But they're not in the same league as me. Mind you, I don't want to boast,' he continued, blinking round at the grinning faces. 'I just want to point out that I'm better than anyone else in the Remove.'

'We all know how modest you are,' said Huree.

'But I don't believe in false modesty,' declared the Owl. 'If you're as good as I am, then you might as well say so. Anyway, the proof of the pudding is in the eating. Just let me have one over, Wharton. That's all I need. After that you'll keep me at it. After all, hat tricks are hat tricks.'

'Oh, my only summer bonnet!' exclaimed Bob.

'As I was saying, Wharton. Just let me have one over. I know you're not much good at judging form, otherwise you'd have put me in the team before now, but you'll be pleased when the wickets go down. Mind you, I don't guarantee a hat trick. I may only take two——'

'Okay. I'm convinced,' said Harry. 'We can afford to chuck away an over as well as a wicket. I'll let you bowl one, and if you do take a wicket, I'll let you carry on for as long as you like.'

'Good,' said Bunter. 'I say, we must make sure that Quelch comes and watches. I want him to see I'm a good all-rounder—a brilliant bat and a deadly bowler. It'll make quite a difference. I bet my report will say that I haven't done too well in class—you know what a down he's got on me, but he won't be able to make out that I'm not good at games.' There was another burst of laughter, and Bunter blinked disdainfully through his specs. 'Cackle away! You'll be laughing on the other side of your silly faces after tomorrow.'

The bell rang for prep, and as Toddy made his way to his study, he said to Bunter, 'Done your lines yet?'

'Lines! Blow lines! I haven't had time to do them, and I'm not going to. Why should I?'

'You'll be in detention tomorrow afternoon,' Toddy pointed out.

Billy Bunter gave him a fat wink. 'We'll see,' he said.

Chapter 29

Bunter All Over!

At the end of morning school, Mr Quelch gave the Owl a long, hard look. 'You have not yet handed in your lines, Bunter. Where are they?'

'Oh, I—er——'

'Have you done them, Bunter?'

'Oh, sir, no, I——'

'Very well then, Bunter. You will do them in detention this afternoon.'

'But you see, Mr Quelch——'

'That is quite enough!' rapped his form master.

'But—but I'm playing cricket this afternoon, sir,' explained the fat Owl. 'I—I'm playing for the form against the fourth. The—the form's relying on me.'

Mr Quelch's eyebrows shot up. 'You are in the team, Bunter?' he said, astonished.

'Yes, Mr Quelch. Wharton picked me yester-day—put my name on the list in the Rag. I've—I've been practising ever since you spoke to me in your study. I'm—I'm really pretty good now.'

'Indeed?' said Quelch, drily. 'If that is true, Bunter, than I'm pleased to hear it. I shall be delighted to make at least one good comment on your report. So you've been practising hard?'

'Been sticking to it like glue,' declared Billy Bunter. 'I've spent every minute I could spare down at the net. I—I expect that's why Wharton picked me for the side.'

'Very well, Bunter. We shall say no more about detention this afternoon, but I shall want those lines by the day after tomorrow. If you are trying to change your ways, then I must encourage you. You may go.'

'Thank you, sir!' said Bunter, and trundled out of the form room just as the bell went for lunch.

'Don't over do it, fat man,' said Bob Cherry as they went into the dining room. 'If you pack too much stodge inside yourself, you won't be able to knock up that century——'

'Or take a hat trick,' said Frank. 'Remember we're relying on you to win the match for us.'

'Yah!' sneered Bunter, as there was a howl of laughter. 'You'll see what I can do—you'll be apologising before the day's out.'

Several helpings later, he got up regretfully from the table. Although he had done well, he hadn't done quite as well as he had hoped. He had a feeling that there was an empty corner in his capacious stomach that badly needed filling.

As he rolled towards the stairs, Bob Cherry overtook him. 'Hurry up, old thing,' he said. 'You'd better get changed.'

'Won't be a tick,' said the Owl, as Bob hurried off to the playing field.

'Where's Bunter?' demanded Harry.

'I've just seen him. He was last out of the dining room as usual. He's gone off to change. I should think he'll be here in a minute or two.'

They hung around for some time, and then, as the fourth form team appeared, Harry looked at his watch. 'What the thump can he be up to?'

'He can't be in the tuckshop,' remarked Johnny. 'He gave the cash to Quelch.'

'He might have had another postal order,' suggested Frank.'

'I say,' said the Bounder. 'He didn't get a letter, but Mauly got a parcel.'

'Even that fat villain wouldn't have helped himself to Mauly's grub,' said Frank.

'Oh, no? Not even if it had jam in it?'

'And did it?' asked Johnny.

'Yes. I saw it in Mauly's study. It was a seven pound jar.'

Although Harry was exasperated, he laughed. 'What's the use of trying to help that burbling fool?' he said. 'Perhaps Temple will let us play a substitute and replace him if Bunter turns up.'

However, the Owl didn't roll onto the field. The Remove fielded, and Hurree Jamset Ram Singh, Tom Brown and Squiff bowled in turn, making hay of the fourth form wickets. The fourth form's innings lasted one hour fifty minutes but they did manage a total of over a hundred when they were all out.

They all went back into the pavilion for drinks. 'Where can that fool be?' asked Bob Cherry. 'He can't have had his snout into jam for all this time.'

'He's last man in, said Harry. 'There'll be plenty of time for him to turn up.'

'Hallo, hallo, hallo!' exclaimed Bob. 'Here's Mauly. Anything disappeared from your study, Mauly?'

'Yaas!'

'It wouldn't have been jam, would it?'

'Yaas.'

'Seen Bunter?'

'Not since I kicked him. Found him in his study,' explained Lord Mauleverer. 'I mean to say, I wouldn't have minded if he had some, but trying to filch the whole jar is a bit much, don't you think?

'Ha, ha, ha!'

'Come on, Bob,' said Harry, strapping on his pads. 'We're opening.'

The Remove team was far better than the fourth form's, and their innings lasted quite a long time, but still the Owl didn't appear. The score was ninety for six when Mr Quelch appeared on the scene. He had not forgotten that Bunter was to be in the team. He looked around sharply, but failed to spot an ample figure in bursting flannels.

'How is the game going, Wharton?' he asked.

'We're almost up to their total, Mr Quelch, and we've still got five wickets in hand.'

'Excellent, Wharton. And how has Bunter shaped? I'm quite interested in his performance.'

'Oh!' It was an awkward question. 'We—that is, Bunter's last man in. He—he won't be wanted for some time—if at all.'

'And what was he like when you were fielding?'

'Oh!' said Harry, 'He——'

Quelch fixed his gimlet eye on Harry as his voice trailed away. It was quite obvious that the captain of the Remove was reluctant to reply. 'He did field, Wharton?'

'Well, no, sir,' said Harry. 'I'm afraid we had to play a substitute.'

'Then he has not put in an appearance?'

'I—I imagine that something came up—something's delayed him,' stammered Harry.

Mr Quelch stared at him. 'When did you last see him?'

'At lunch,' said Harry.

'And have you any idea of where he might be?'

'I'm afraid not, Mr Quelch.'

Mr Quelch said no more. There was no need. His expression said it all. He watched the game for a few minutes, and then he returned to the school.

'Bunter's for the high jump,' remarked Bob.

'Serves him right!' grunted Johnny. 'The fat slacker!'

Mr Quelch's brow was thunderous. He had been prepared to revise his opinion of the fat Owl if he really was making an effort, but it seemed that the boy was a hopeless case. Nevertheless, Quelch was a fair man. Although he was almost certain that Bunter had been slacking again, there was just a remote possibility that there was some explanation.

He looked into the Rag and saw Skinner and Snoop talking together. 'Can you tell me where Bunter is?'

'In his study, Mr Quelch,' said Skinner. 'I saw him there a few minute ago,' and he grinned.

'Thank you,' replied Mr Quelch, wondering why the two boys thought it funny that Bunter should be in his study. He mounted the stairs and strode along the Remove passage, quickening his pace as he heard a groan.

'Oooo-er! Oh, lor'! Ooooh!'

Mr Quelch opened the door. 'Bless my soul!' he exclaimed.

A rotund form was stretched out in the study arm-chair. The fat Owl's face was ghastly. It was pale green, and he looked as he might have done had he been on a Channel crossing on a very rough day. His fat, sticky paws were pressed to his extensive waist-coat, and he was groaning and gurgling.

'Bless my soul!' said Quelch again, but his face grew stern as he saw why Bunter was prostrate. There was an enormous jam jar on the table, and by its side, a tablespoon. Quelch looked at the almost empty pot. 'You wretched boy!' he rasped.

'Oooo-er!' Bunter was quite unable to rise from the chair. He gave a lack-lustre blink at his form master.

'So this is why you weren't on the cricket field! I excused you from detention because you were to play, and now I find you in this disgraceful condition!'

'Oooogh!'

'You have been gorging yourself with jam——'

'M—m—my—Oooh-er!'

'Which I am certain belongs to some other boy——'

'Groo-agh!'

'And you have made yourself positively ill because of your greed.'

'Oooo-grooo!'

'Whose jam was it, Bunter?'

'Oooogh! It—it wasn't Mauly's, sir,' groaned Bunter. 'It—it was mine. That is, he—he gave it to me. He did—didn't kick me when he caught me scoffing it. At least, he—he understood that it—it was only a joke, sir—groooogh!'

'Wooooh! I—I don't feel well.'

'You have gone too far, Bunter! I have made up my mind. Your end of term report——'

'But—oooh! I—I really was going to play in the team, honestly I was. Only meant to sample it. Just to let Mauly know if it was up to scratch—oooo-er! I—I—I'm terribly keen on crick—crick—cricket, sir. Ooo—oooh! I—I say, sir, I—I don't think that I feel very well. wooooch!'

You have made no improvement Bunter. Your report will be accompanied by a letter suggesting that your father should take you away from Greyfriars. You are a very stupid and greedy boy! This is the last straw!'

'Grooo!'

'Pah!' snapped Mr Quelch, and stalked out of the study.

Billy Bunter hardly noticed him go. He felt as if earthquakes and tornadoes were battling within his podgy circumference. He was past caring about anything. He went on moaning and groaning and gurgling, and when the rest of the Remove came in, he was still at it.

Chapter 30

The Last Straw

'The die is cast!' said Toddy.

'Eh? What do you mean?' asked Billy Bunter.

'Your fate is settled.'

'Oh!' grunted the downcast Owl.

'The game's up, fatty.'

'Beast!'

'Quelch is fed up to the back teeth with you. You'll

be waving goodbye to Greyfriars at the end of term. Serve you right.'

'Oh, really, Toddy!' protested Bunter.

He felt that he'd just been unfortunate. He hadn't intended to miss that match. It hadn't been his fault. It was the jam's. He'd only meant to sample it, but it had turned out to be particularly delicious. Having started, he'd been unable to stop. And surely someone who felt so ill deserved a bit of sympathy, but all he'd got from those beasts in the Remove were hard words. Anyway, Mauly ought to have had a bit of the blame. It had been his jam, hadn't it?

And on Monday, he'd probably sealed his fate when he'd told Quelch that the plague of 1665 had been caused by jam. Quelch had stared, and everyone had expected the thunder to roll, but nothing had happened. There had been an icy calm. It was as if he'd not been in the form room at all.

That evening Bunter had made a desperate effort to do some work during prep. He had prepared his Latin translation for the next day, but it was wasted. His unaccustomed store of knowledge had remained bottled up.

'Look what happened today, Toddy,' he said, morosely. 'I did my prep, didn't I? And then Quelch goes and passes me over. Didn't ask me to translate one word. Need not have bothered to slog away at the beastly Latin.'

'Quelch isn't a magician,' Toddy pointed out. 'How could he have guessed that you'd done a spot of work for once in your life?'

'Yah!' Bunter rolled out of the study. It was time for tea, and his fat little legs trundled him along to study no 1.

'Oh, it's you.' Harry Wharton reached for a cushion, but seeing the Owl's glum face, he dropped it.

The gloom lifted a little as Bunter spotted the cake

on the table. 'I say, you fellows,' he said, his eyes glued to it, 'that looks like a decent enough cake. Mind you, it's nothing like the cakes we get at Bunter Court, but I dare say it'll taste all right. I could manage a slice. Give you my considered opinion.'

'Oh, all right,' said Frank.

Bunter carved himself a piece, thoughtfully leaving almost half of it on the plate. Five fellows looked expressively at the cake, and even more expressively at Bunter. The Owl didn't notice. He was deep in cake.

'I say, you fellows.' His voice was muffled. 'It really looks as if I'm for it. I don't understand Quelch. He's always been down on me.'

'I wonder why,' remarked Johnny.

'It's prejudice,' said Bunter sadly. 'Teachers often get prejudices, don't they? Stuffed with them. Well, there's no point in trying to please a beak when he's prejudiced. I don't pretend that I'm perfect——'

'You don't!' gasped Johnny Bull.

'Why not?' enquired Frank.

'Well, none of us is perfect. I don't claim I am, but I'm a cut above you lot, but Quelch can't see it. Don't want to. None so blind as those who won't see,' added Bunter, bitterly. 'I could understand it if he was down on one of you, but is he? No. It's me he's down on. It's queer, but there it is. Teachers are funny—they're not like other people.'

Billy Bunter munched his cake as the Famous Five gazed at him. 'It looks as if I'm going to get a bad report after all. Tain't fair, not after the work I've put in. That means you won't see me next term. I wouldn't be surprised if you all get a good report while Quelch gives me a rotten one. There ain't no justice in Greyfriars.'

'Oh, crumbs!'

'Maybe Quelch will have something to remember me by,' said Bunter, darkly. 'I've done my best —you're all witnesses to that, and it's made no difference. Still, worms do turn.'

'What? What are you up to?'

'Oh! Nothing! Anyway, even if I am, I'm not going to tell you,' went on the fat Owl. 'Least said, soonest mended. I might make Quelch feel sorry for himself, and I might not. That would be telling. I don't want to get a head's flogging, do I? No, I'll have to keep it dark. Don't want to ask for trouble.'

'Keep what dark?' asked Bob.

Bunter put a fat finger to the side of his nose. 'Sh!' he said warningly. 'Haven't said a word.'

'But you have,' said Frank.

'I'm not going to say any more. It might get round, and I don't want Quelch to know what's coming to him,' explained Bunter. 'But he might get a surprise tomorrow afternoon. He's going to walk across to Highcliffe to watch the match, isn't he? And if he's going to walk, then he'll go by way of the footpath across Courtfield Common, won't he?'

'I expect so. It's a good short cut. But what on earth——?'

'Well, you know the wood right in the middle of the common, don't you?' grinned the fat Owl. 'The footpath goes right through it. There are branches thick over the path—thick as anything, they are. No one would spot a chap who was tucked up in one of those trees.'

'What are you on about?' said Bob. 'Are you saying that you're going to hide in a tree?'

'Oh, didn't say so, did I? I'm not going to say any more. I can't trust you to keep your mouths shut, but when Quelch comes along under those branches, he may get a nasty surprise or he may not. An athletic fellow——'

'So you are not going to be there, my dear Bunter?' asked Hurree Singh.

Bunter ignored him. 'As I was saying, someone like me may be up there with a bag of soot or——'

'A bag of soot!' yelled Johnny.

'At this time of the year?' said Frank. 'Where are you going to get soot?'

Bunter looked cunning. 'The head's got a garden, hasn't he? There are roses in that garden, and the gardener always has soot. Uses it on them. I've got it all worked out.'

'You're off your head,' roared Bob. 'You can't drop soot on Quelch!'

'Stop shouting!' snapped Bunter. 'I told you, I've got to keep it dark. I don't want to be flogged before I leave, do I? It'll be quite a shock when it lands on Quelch's head, won't it? Hee, hee, hee!'

'You're a maniac!' said Harry. 'Quelch will skin you alive.'

'Tee, hee, hee. He's not going to see me, is he? I'm going to be hidden in the tree, and his eyes and nose and mouth are going to be bunged up with soot. Hee, hee, hee!'

'Don't do it, fat man,' said Frank.

'You can't!' exclaimed Bob.

'Can't I?' jeered Bunter. 'I'm jolly well going to give Quelch something to remember me by. I've slogged away, done everything I could to please him, and I'm still going to get a bad report. 'Tain't fair.' He began to chuckle again. 'By the time you get back from Highcliffe, it'll all be over. Tee, hee, hee! The news will be all over the school. He'll have come stumbling in, black from head to foot——'

'Look here, you potty porpoise——'

'Got any more cake?'

'No, you dustbin!'

'You get pretty poor teas in this study these days,' said Bunter, with a disdainful sniff. 'Must go. I think I'll have a word with Mauly.' He rolled away, leaving the Famous Five looking uneasily at each other.

'He can't mean it, can he?' asked Frank.

'He can't be serious,' said Bob. 'It's all talk. It must be.'

145

'He'll never walk all the way,' remarked Harry. 'It's well over a mile.'

'And then our fat friend will still have to climb a tree,' said Hurree. 'I cannot see him doing that.'

'He's a lazy slacker,' Johnny said. 'He'll never do it.'

'Of course he won't,' agreed Harry.

Although they dismissed Bunter and his threats from their minds, the fat Owl rolled on, his shoulders shaking with mirth as he pictured the blackened Quelch returning to school on the following afternoon.

Chapter 31
Two in Ambush

'This will do.'

Billy Bunter looked up at gnarled oak tree. He thought he could manage to climb it, and so he parked his bag of soot in the fork of the tree.

He had left Greyfriars as soon as lunch was over, and had trundled across Courtfield Common to the little wood in the middle of it. Although it was a bright day, the thick branches of the trees that met over the footpath blotted out the sunshine.

He took a deep breath, and after several attempts, managed to scramble up the oak. He grabbed the soot, and crawled along a sturdy branch until he was directly above the path.

'Tee, hee, hee!' he giggled, as he stretched himself out, sure that his bulk was concealed by the leafy tree. If things went according to plan, he'd be able to drop the soot on top of Quelch and get away without being caught.

It was so comfortable that he had to pinch himself to keep awake. Then, at last, he heard approaching footsteps.

'That's him,' he said, grinning, and blinked down. Carefully, he parted the foliage, and then he gasped.

'Crikey!' It wasn't Quelch coming along that lonely footpath! It wasn't Quelch at all. Bunter's fat little heart nearly stopped beating as he saw who it was. He knew that stubbly face with its red-rimmed eyes and twisted nose. It was the villain who had attacked him!

The man was coming along hurriedly, and the Owl held his breath, watching anxiously for him to pass on and disappear, but it didn't happen. Nosey Jenkins came to a halt, looked back, and listened intently. Then he stepped off the footpath, and hid himself behind the same massive oak tree that Bunter was in.

He vanished from view, leaving the fat junior staring. There was hardly a sound after he had disappeared, and only the faint sound of a rustling leaf told Bunter that he was still there.

'Beast!' hissed the Owl. His plans might be ruined. Quelch would certainly appear before long, but he could hardly go into action with that villain around.

At first Bunter couldn't think what the man was doing there, but then it slowly dawned on him that he was probably lying in wait for someone. He must have spotted his victim coming across the common, and had gone into hiding so that he could take him by surprise. 'Oh, brandy balls!' he breathed, as he realised that he was almost certainly going to be the sole witness of a violent scene. The sight of Nosey Jenkins terrified him. The thought that he might come face to face with him again made his heart pound so loudly that he was afraid that it might be heard.

He gave a little start as the sound of footsteps came to his ears. Someone else was coming along the footpath. Bunter shuddered. From the bottom of his fat heart he wished that he had never thought of this masterly scheme of paying Quelch back.

Quelch! Bunter clapped a fat paw to his mouth. That's who was coming. That villain was going to take his revenge on Quelch. 'Oh, lor'!' breathed the Owl.

A moment later, a tall, angular figure came into view. Mr Quelch was striding along, his walking stick tucked beneath his arm. As Quelch passed beneath the tree, there was a loud rustle. Nosey Jenkins leaped from cover, sprang at Quelch, and grabbed him from behind. Quelch went flying, dropping his walking stick.

'Oh!' groaned Bunter.

Quelch was on his back, and Nosey Jenkins was on top of him, with one knee firmly planted on his chest.

'Gotcher!' snarled Nosey. 'Got you, you interfering cuss.'

Mr Quelch, utterly helpless, stared up at that ugly, threatening face. He made a great effort to throw off his assailant, but Nosey clung on.

'I'll show you! I'll give you what for. I owe you something, don't I? You done me. Well, now it's my turn to do you.' He reached for his cudgel. 'I'll crack your nut!'

'You—you brute!' stammered Mr Quelch.

Nosey brandished his stick. 'See this!' he jeered. 'Just you take a good look at it. It'll be the last thing that you'll see,' and he gave Quelch a savage grin.

'You won't get away with it,' said Quelch.

'Oh, no? Who's to know? There's just you and me, and you won't be able to talk.' Nosey lifted the stick in the air.

The Owl peered down. No one could call him a hero. He wasn't even plucky, but the sight of Quelch in danger made him act. If he'd thought, he'd have done nothing, but he didn't stop to think.

He went into action. He parted the leaves, clutched the branch for a moment, and then he let go.

Nosey Jenkins was taken completely by surprise.

Nosey Jenkins was taken completely by surprise.

One moment there he was, his victim pinned down, ready to crack Quelch's nut, and then he was sprawling on the grass, dazed and dizzy and almost stunned by the weight that had dropped on him.

As Bunter rolled over onto the ground, he grabbed Nosey so that Quelch was able to scramble to his feet. In a flsash, his form master seized the cudgel, and hurled it into the bushes. He grabbed his walking stick, and stood over the man. Suddenly, he realised that it was Bunter who had rescued him. 'Bless my soul!' he exclaimed. 'It's you, Bunter.'

Bunter sat up. He gasped and spluttered. 'Ooooh!'

Mr Quelch glanced at the tree. 'Goodness gracious, boy. You were up there!'

Bunter blinked anxiously, thinking of that bag of soot. 'Oh, not me, sir,' he said planting his glasses more firmly on his button of a nose. 'Oh, no, sir! I—I wasn't. I—I——'

'I think you were, Bunter,' said Mr Quelch. He saw Nosey Jenkins move, and he prodded him again with his walking stick.

'Well, sir, if I was, I didn't mean to be. I wasn't doing nothing wrong, Mr Quelch, really I wasn't. I—er—I was climbing a tree, sir. I—I—I like climbing trees. Often do it when I'm on my own.' He couldn't understand the look on Quelch's face. Could his form master really have guessed what he was going to do? It wouldn't have surprised him. Quelch seemed to have an uncanny knack of knowing what was going on. 'I—that is——'

'There is no need to say more, Bunter,' said Quelch. Bunter was reassured by his tone. For once, he wasn't being barked at. 'I am very grateful to you. You have saved me from an unpleasant experience.' He jabbed at Nosey again.

'Oh, oh! I—I—er—I wasn't afraid of that brute, sir. I—I couldn't let him thump you with his stick—I—I mean, I couldn't let him crack your nut open and not do anything, sir, so—so I—I jumped on him, Mr Quelch. I—I—don't think that I was afraid, sir.'

Mr Quelch smiled. It was quite clear to him that Bunter had been scared out of his fat wits, but in spite of that, he had somehow managed to screw up his courage, and had literally weighed in on his form master's side.

Mr Quelch was well aware that he might have been very seriously hurt and that only Bunter's arrival had saved him from injury—the boy he had decided must leave Greyfriars. Until now, he had been unable to think of anything that he could have said in Bunter's favour—now the situation was different.

He smiled again. 'You have been very courageous, Bunter.'

'Oh!'

'And I want you to know just how grateful I am.'

'Oh!' gasped Bunter again, hardly able to take it in. Was Quelch actually praising him?

'I shall certainly refer to it in my end of term report.'

'Thank you, Mr Quelch.'

'And I shall not advise your father to remove you from Greyfriars.'

'Oh, thank you, sir.'

'And I shall hope to see your general conduct improve.'

'Oh, it will,' said Bunter, earnestly.

'And now go as fast as you can to the police station and report this incident. Ask them to send a constable as soon as possible. I want this man to be taken into custody.'

'Will—will you be all right, Mr Quelch?'

'I think so,' said Mr Quelch.

Billy Bunter rolled off, his face beaming from side to side. Nosey Jenkins remained where he was while Mr Quelch jabbed him yet again with his walking stick. The prospect of being locked up by the police seemed less terrifying than the prospect of being whacked by that irate school master.

Chapter 32

The Reward for Valour

'I say, you fellows!'

'Hallo, hallo, hallo!'

Bunter beamed. 'Everything's all right.'

'So it is,' agreed Bob Cherry. 'You ought to have stirred yourself and come over to see the match.'

'Did you win?'

'Beat them by fifteen runs,' said Harry Wharton, happily.

'Is that all?' said the Owl. 'It would have been different if I'd been there.'

'How right you are,' remarked Hurree Singh.

'It was a first-class game,' said Bob, enthusiastically. 'Highcliffe were good, but we managed to pull it off. I wish Quelch had got there sooner, though. He didn't turn up until the end.'

'Seen him, have you?' asked Bunter, casually. 'Did he happen to mention that I saved his life this afternoon?'

'Eh?'

'What?'

'Tell us another.'

'I think he might have said. It's a bit much. He ought to have said. After all, it's not something that happens every day of the week, is it?'

Bob grinned. 'Not exactly, fat man.'

'What are you on about?' asked Johnny Bull.

'I told you. I saved Quelch's life. He seemed quite pleased.'

'I bet he was if it happened.'

'But I told you——'

'Heard the latest?' said Skinner, as a group of Remove fellows entered the Rag. 'It's his best yet. Bunter's saved Quelch's life.'

'Ha, ha, ha!'

'He'll want to join the SAS.'

'Or the President's bodyguard,' said Fisher T Fish.

'Oh, really, Fishy!'

'He didn't look any different when he turned up at the end of the match,' said the Bounder.

'He wouldn't have been there at all if it hadn't been for me,' said Bunter, proudly. 'Not that I want to boast. But still, I rushed headlong into danger—didn't think of myself——'

'Ha, ha, ha!'

'Faced a desperate villain who was armed to the teeth——'

'Keep it up,' urged Bob.

'And so I saved his life, so he ain't got a down on me now that I've shaved his wife—no, no, saved his life. I'm going to get a jolly good report. Mind you, I deserve it. He's begged me to stay on. He put his hand on my shoulder and said that I was gallant, a credit to the form, a future captain of the school, that's what he said.'

'Oh, yes?' said Johnny. 'I can just hear him.'

'Those were his very words. He said I was gallant, and that he wished you lot were more like me. He said I was a shining example to you all. The school needs people like me—those were his very words.'

'And how did you save his life? asked Hurree, curiously.

'That bloke who got hold of Quelch near Red-clyffe—the one who jumped on me, well, he pounced on Quelch. Just like a tiger he was, so I sprang on him like—like——'

'A hippopotamus?' suggested Toddy.

'Ha, ha, ha!'

'Shut up!' hooted the Owl. 'I sprang on him like a lion, and bore him——'

'That sounds right,' said Smithy. 'Bunter would bore anyone.'

'Right,' said Bob. 'Okay. What happened after that?'

'Listen! I bore him to the earth. Had him in a grip of iron. Disregarded his gleaming knife. Pinned him down although I could see it was about a foot long, and as sharp as a razor. Didn't give it a second thought——'

'Didn't know you ever had one,' said Bob.

'Thought only of Quelch. Didn't care about myself. Like I said, I sprang on him so that he couldn't crack Quelch's nut with his cudgel. You should have seen it. There was a great knob on the end. Missed me by a fraction of an inch as I sprang on him. I would have been brained——'

'Impossible, my dear Bunter!'

'I had a jolly narrow escape. I felt the wind of the bullet as it sped by——'

'I thought he'd got a cudgel, not a gun,' said Smithy.

'Oh—oh, did I say that? Slip of the tongue. No. The cudgel, that's what I was on about. You should have seen him. He had Quelch by the throat——'

'With one hand?'

'No, no. With both—held him in a grip of steel——'

'What a guy!' remarked Bob. 'A knife in one hand, a cudgel in the other, and Quelch held down with the rest——'

'Don't be ridiculous, Cherry!' snapped Bunter. 'You—you weren't listening properly. The fact is——'

'Forget about the facts,' said Bob. 'They're not in your line. Now, get on with the story.'

'Ha, ha, ha!'

'You fellows don't believe me,' roared Bunter, indignantly.

'Whatever makes you think that?' asked Frank.

'Well, I'm telling you that I did do it. I got the villain and I saved Quelch's life——'

'Jolly good, fat man,' said Smithy. 'Got another

fairy story for us?'

'Yah! I done it just like I told you,' Bunter insisted. 'I saved his life like Cromwell saved Nelson in the oak tree.' He looked annoyed at the laughter. 'I did, I tell you. Anyhow, I did it all by myself. I'd got him on the ground, helpless at my feet, and that's when old Quelch put his hand on my head——'

'And the other one was on your shoulder, wasn't it?' asked Bob.

'And what was he doing with the third?'

'Don't be stupid, Bull,' snorted Bunter. 'Well, there he was, senseless at my feet, and that was when——' He broke off. 'Oh, crikey,' he said as the tall figure of Mr Quelch appeared at the door of the Rag.

All the juniors looked at their form master. They expected that the volcano would erupt but, much to their surprise, Quelch had a smile on his face.

'Bunter,' he said.

'Oh! Oh, yes, sir.'

Mr Quelch walked into the common room, and held out a large tin. 'Bunter,' he said. 'I have brought you a small gift, not as a reward for your courageous behaviour this afternoon, but as a token of my good opinion of you.'

'Oh, Mr Quelch. Thank you, sir.'

The juniors looked amazed. It hardly seemed possible, but could there be a grain of truth in the fat Owl's story?

'Excuse me, Mr Quelch,' said Harry Wharton, 'but has Bunter done anything special this afternoon?'

'He has indeed,' said Mr Quelch. 'I was attacked by a villainous tramp, and Bunter, who fortunately had climbed a tree at that very spot, jumped down and disabled him. I have already expressed my gratitude to Bunter, and I am pleased to do so again in front of you all.' Quelch gave Bunter a smile, and left the Rag.

'Well, my best bowler!' exclaimed Bob. 'Wonder's will never cease. I bet you didn't get round to telling

Quelch just why you were up that tree, fat man.'

'Ha, ha, ha!'

'Funny that Quelch forgot to mention that the brute had got a knife that was a foot long,' remarked Skinner.

'Well, he was in a bit of a state,' said Bunter. 'I don't suppose he noticed. I was all right. I was as cool as cowcumber—I mean I was as cow as a coolcumber. No, no, I—I mean—I say, you fellows, I wonder what's in this tin?'

He forced open the lid, and gave a gasp of delight. It was full of toffees. He blinked, and he beamed, and then he grabbed a handful.

'I say, you fellows.' His voice was a little muffled. 'These toffees are smashing! Good old Quelch. He really knows how to treat someone who has saved his life. He's not such a bad old stick, is he?'

There was a burst of laughter, and Bunter went on, 'I say, have some. There are lots and lots and lots. I say, he ain't such a beast after all. Oooogh! Groogh! Worooh!' Bunter choked, coughed, and then recovered. 'Urrgh! They're terrific. Have some.'

Bunter was a happy and sticky Owl that evening. The knowledge that Quelch had relented and he was going to be able to return to Greyfriars next term was pleasing, but the toffees pleased him even more.